Thursday Nights: Short Fiction

Thursday Nights: Short Fiction

Celebrating 40 years of Tindal Street Fiction Group

Curated by Rob Ganley, Alan Beard and
Mick Scully

First published in 2023
by Tindal Street Fiction Group
www.tindalstreetfictiongroup.com

The Tanks by Anthony Ferner was first published
in the Irish Times – our thanks are due for permission
to republish in this anthology.

Paperback ISBN: 978-0-9528246-2-6
Ebook ISBN: 978-0-9528246-3-3

Cover artwork: Sicco Hesselmans

Printed in the United Kingdom by IngramSpark

Tindal Street Fiction Group
Thursday Nights
All endorsements provided by successful former group members

'A wonderful collection about ordinary, intimate and forgotten lives told with warmth and verve from some of the best Birmingham writers. I loved it.'
Kit de Waal, author of *My Name is Leon, The Trick to Time, Without Warning and Only Sometimes* and others

'Once a member of this eclectic writing group, I had almost forgotten how much hot, pure talent is bubbling out of Birmingham on Thursday Nights. This collection is gold. Pure gold.'
Amanda Smyth, author of *Black Rock, A Kind of Eden* and *Fortune*

'Tindal Street Fiction Group has long been a bright star in UK literature, producing writers as diverse as the city that inspired them. Full of heart and voice and the concerns of the contemporary moment, these stories are proof of a thriving literary scene. If you want first-class fiction look to the UK's second city.'
Julia Bell, author of *Massive* and *Dirty Work*

'This collection from the ever talented writers of TSFG gives us perfectly pitched stories that range across the globe from Cornwall to Delhi and back... A fantastic, unmissable collection.'
Mez Packer, author of *Among Thieves* and *The Game is Altered*

'Like Birmingham, this wonderful collection of short stories is diverse, vibrant and full of warmth. Sometimes whispering, sometimes screaming, forever beguiling – the voices that have emerged from TSFG have always been the most compelling.'
Ryan Davis, author of *27*

'Those Thursday nights... Before there were writing courses in every city, TSFG offered itself as Birmingham's university of creative writing and helped shape so many of us. And what a pleasure to read the fascinating, high quality stories still flowering from the workshop. The stories are varied in tone, setting and subject matter as befits our inclusive Second City, each unfurling a complete world of its own. A really excellent anthology.'
Annie Murray, author of *Chocolate Girls, The Doorstep Child, Birmingham Friends* and many more

'A beautiful and varied collection of stories that root the reader in Birmingham and beyond. For forty years, TSFG have nurtured each others' craft and careers. This is a collection that celebrates a writing group at its best: telling intimate, poignant stories filled with memorable characters and expert world building... these stories grip the reader and show us unexpected moments that reveal a character's longing.'
Sidura Ludwig, author of *Holding My Breath* and *You Are Not What We Expected*

'The Tindal Street Fiction Group has helped to launch the careers of a host of successful authors... It's a list that must be the envy of many of the most illustrious M.A. in Creative Writing courses in the country... Drawing on the work of the current membership, it is a worthy showcase for the group's talents... Highly recommended!'
Charles Wilkinson, author of *The Pain Tree and Other Stories,* and others

'Assured, and at times, brilliant stories to lose yourself in. TSFG transports you to JFK, Italy, Wales, London, Proper London, India, San Francisco, St Ives and more with tales of love in a time of war, travel, both physical and emotional, the call of the sea and the heart, quests for identity and understanding... the awkwardness of not fitting in and the lies we tell to do so. A powerful collection from the Midlands.'
Garrie Fletcher, writer and one-third of Birmingham-based publisher Floodgate. His work is in *Digbeth Stories* (Floodgate, 2023), *Submerged* and *Night Swimming* (both Mantle Lane Press).

In memory of Joel Lane, a much-loved and hugely talented member of Tindal Street Fiction Group, who is still greatly missed by all who knew him, ten years on since his untimely death in 2013.

CONTENTS

CONTENTS

This book celebrates the 40th anniversary of Tindal Street Fiction Group. For the 20th and 30th anniversaries, current and former members were invited to contribute to anthologies (*Going the Distance*, 2003; *The Sea in Birmingham*, 2013) and the books were kind of 'Greatest Hits' compilations. This time round we still wanted to produce an anthology of work to mark such an important milestone, but decided to do something different, something simpler and perhaps more satisfying: showcase the group as it stands now.

So, all current full members were invited to submit self-selected and self-edited pieces (either stories or novel extracts) for publication. The only criterion was a 5,000 word limit. All but one of the full members happily obliged and all but one of the submitted pieces were workshopped by the group. Thus, the texts here truly highlight the work of our members and give a snapshot of the group in action.

Alan Beard
Tindal Street Fiction Group Secretary
and member since 1985

Forty years, once a fortnight, maybe 20 meetings a year, so that's around 800 meetings and what did we talk about? Other people's writing, of course. You get to look forward to hearing about the country and the city, the past and the dangerous present, love and longing, disappointment, spite, funny stuff: stories. You listen as intently as if you were a child tucked up in bed being read a bedtime story, thumb in your mouth. Weirdly, you're an adult being read to, and it's a precious space of concentration and surprise. Except you will already have read the text and scribbled notes in the margin of the printout – so it's not entirely new, but there are always fresh notes introduced, things you missed first time, maybe new errors, but always new felicities. *I really liked that bit.*

And once or twice a year you might get the chance to present your own work – put your own precious story through the wringer. *That's an archaism, surely.* And then it's all about you, for one night only. How could I improve this piece? Is it back to the drawing board or straight into the recycling bin? How will I remember everything that everyone said? When I don't even agree that that point was valid. I had something different in mind. Writers groups test and expose your intentions. *No, that wasn't what I meant.*

You read it out loud – in the process realising some more of your errors, repetitions, awkward sentences – and then you must filter out the comments, process them, deciding which you must work on and which you can let go. Will you rewrite it immediately or let it stew? Lots of comments, mostly consensual, but sometimes contradictory. It's helpful to hear sensitive, knowledgeable critiquing about endings, about duff dialogue, dodgy syntax.

There's something to be said for a collective knowledge in an experienced writing group – someone knows all about the Beatles, someone all about drugs, another about crime, someone about birds and classical music, someone else nineteenth century novels, the countryside in Hardy's day, the probation service, the law, film, party politics, Dutch, Spanish, Italian, French, German so beware – everything you thought you could get away with by blagging – about a type of tree or a flower in bloom – did you get it right? Careful readers will spot the errors. A group of them allows you some confidence.

I must admit I've pitched some very miscellaneous pieces to the group – short stories, memoirs, chapters of a novel in endless progress – and every time I benefited. Because I was enabled to see how others might read what I'd written, when I could only see it from my own blindfolded point of view. I foolishly thought it made complete sense, my intentions for it must have been clear. But they weren't always. I'm slapdash, where some people are meticulous. I go right up to the deadline and offer something provisional, not quite finished, so of course the process of feedback helps me finish the damned thing.

I was there at the beginning, I started it off, in fact, by gathering some other people together who were writing and wanted to improve. And I wasn't their teacher. No one was the teacher, there was never a teacher. We were all at the same level, with the same aims, to write better and maybe get published. Peers. Rivals in a sense, but all with different approaches, different ideals. We weren't really competing with each other in striving to attract the attention of editors. We were dogged triers and strugglers, we hoped we were contenders. And everyone got something published. Some went on to make a dent in the world of publishing: Julia Bell, Joel Lane, Kit de Waal, Annie Murray, Amanda Smyth, Luke Brown – a roll call of names passing through, changing over the years, sometimes every few months, but all remembered with pride and affection.

And successful authors don't just go off and forget their roots. Some stay: Gaynor Arnold still reads and writes for us (as well as for herself), Alan Beard brings his honed stories to us, hones them some more and then gets them published, and Mick Scully still mines that criminal, dodgy seam in the geology of Birmingham's underground.

There are fourteen strong stories in this anthology. I know because – again, sorry – I was there. I heard them all when they were read. I enjoyed reading them all – and you will too. No, actually, they're all better than when I heard them because like all good writers, these story writers have made improvements, taken on board suggestions, had some time to polish

their pieces till they shine in their different ways. You'll find
that they do.

Alan Mahar
Tindal Street Fiction Group founder in 1983
and former Publishing Director of Tindal Street Press

Thursday Nights: Short Stories

Ashok Patel

Ashok is a Lecturer in biomedical sciences and joined Tindal Street Fiction Group in September 2021. He has written a short play for stage which toured nationally (*Jeevan Saathi; Life partner*), two community plays (*Multicultural* and *Ninety days*), a BBCR4 afternoon play (*Jeevan Saathi; Life partner*), two short stories in anthologies ('Ninety days' in *Dividing Lines* and 'Milly' in *Five stories*) and three short films (*Obsession*, *Chahana* and *Cathy and I*). 'Hotel Shalimar' is based on an incident that happened to him when he was backpacking in India many years ago and is the first story that he read to the Tindal Street Fiction Group. He has found working with the talented and experienced writers in the group invaluable in his writing development.

I watch India pass by through the barred train windows. The heat is relentless and it grips this country like a figure-of-eight knot. Entire rivers vanish leaving behind parched land sighing for monsoon with patches of water around which washerwomen crowd.

Suddenly a globule of red sputum flies out of the carriage narrowly missing me. I stare at the man sitting opposite. He takes out a tobacco paan wrapped in a quarter page of the Hindustan Times with some thread and carefully unwraps it. He takes a bite and offers the rest to me. When I refuse, he wiggles his head in that Indian way and pops it deftly into his mouth. He crumples up the newspaper and nonchalantly throws it out of the window. A slurp is followed by a swallow and then he nudges the mixture to one side of his mouth, forming a lump the size of a small lime. He smiles at me disarmingly revealing reddened stumps of teeth. He wiggles his head again as if to say *don't worry it was never going to hit you. I've done this many times before.*

'What is your good name?' he says.

'Sanjay,' I say.

'Sanjay,' he says, pronouncing it correctly. He lifts one leg onto his seat, dangles an arm on his raised knee and stares directly at me. His wife has her saree drawn over her head with an end pulled across to cover most of her face. Her eyes, clear white with irises stained a deep mahogany, dart in my direction but never make eye contact with me. She is listening intently though I doubt if she understands much English. The tips of her fingers have been dipped in henna, as have the soles of her feet. The rest of her hands and feet are exquisitely adorned with henna patterns and rings wrap the second toe of each foot as a symbol of her marital status.

'From where are you coming? London, or Proper London?' he says. I've had this question fired at me many times on this trip and I know that Indians refer to the UK as London and London as Proper London.

'Proper London,' I say.

'Achchha,' he says, but before he can continue, he is interrupted by a boy who is balancing a heavy plastic tub on his head.

'FantaLimcaThumbsUp,' the boy shouts catching my eye.

He lifts the tub off his head and rests it on his raised knee in one movement. It's filled with ice punctured with brightly coloured bottles of soft drinks.

'Thanda, thanda. Fanta, Limca, Thumbs Up?' the boy singsongs.

'My brother's father-in-law's sister's family live in proper London! Wembalee, Wembalee,' the paan-eater says. His wife turns her face to look directly at me and they both stare at me in expectation.

'I don't know them,' I say as I give the boy ten rupees and take a bottle of Limca. He throws me a smile as I wave away the change. 'I live on the other side of Proper London.'

They both look disappointed and his wife averts her gaze from me once again.

'Are you marry-ed?' he asks.

'No.'

'Why not? What is the matter with you NRIs? You must get marry-ed. There are many girls in India who will marry you because they want to go to Proper London.' I smile at him and continue to look out of the window. Before long he loses interest in me and starts to talk loudly in Hindi to another passenger.

I take out a three-day old Guardian newspaper from my rucksack. The headlines are all about Blair and his first hundred days in power after ousting the Tories. I smile as I think of everyone working away in the lab at UCL, still probably on a high after we'd all helped to vote in the first Labour government in a generation. Most of them had thought it was a great idea when I told them I was off travelling but some wondered if it was the best decision for my research career.

As the train pulls into the station I strap on my backpack, grip my bum bag with one hand and my day bag with the other. There is an undulating noisy horde on the platform as desperate to get on the train as we are to get off. As the train groans to a standstill there is a brief lull in the noise as everyone tenses in readiness like two opposing armies before battle. I nod goodbye to the paan-eater and his wife. The mayhem starts even before the train has completely stopped. The train doors are flung open and a deluge of people shout, shove and claw their way into and out of the train. I push my way through them holding on to my bags. I find some space on the platform away from the frenzy and compose myself. Before long I am surrounded by four rickshaw wallahs.

'Hotel? Hotel?' says one of them.

'Very best hotel?' says another. I ignore them and walk away, letting them know that I'm no push-over. Eventually I follow one of them to his rickshaw, which stands in a line of rickshaws curled around the station like a basking snake.

'Hotel Blue Lagoon, 5 star sir,' the driver says as I climb into his rickshaw.

'No,' I say, having already decided on a cheaper option recommended in the Lonely Planet.

'Take me to Hotel Shalimar.'

'Good price Hotel Blue Lagoon, especial price for you.'

'No, take me to Hotel Shalimar.'

He isn't happy at missing out on the commission that top end hotels give to rickshaw wallahs for bringing in new customers.

'How much?' I ask. He waves his hand and says 'as you like, as you like.'

I ask again but I am drowned out by his rickshaw coughing into life and speeding through the traffic with constantly beeping horn as I hang on tightly.

We arrive at Hotel Shalimar after a twenty-five minute journey including the customary detour.

'How much?' I say climbing out of the rickshaw unsteadily.

'As you like,' the driver says with a smile.

I offer him a 50 rupee note, which is generous for a 20 rupee ride. His smile is quickly replaced by a look of deep offence tinged with anger.

'Don't give me,' he says 'never! Give me 30 pounds.'

'What! That's more than 2000 rupees!' I say, walking away from him.

'OK, give me 10 pounds,' he says. I wave the 50 rupee note at him.

'Never,' he says, turning his head away petulantly like Shah Rukh Khan in this year's film blockbuster Kuch Kuch Hota Hai. A young Indian guy appears from the hotel, takes the 50 rupee note from my hand and slips it in the driver's shirt pocket.

'Challo, challo,' he says ushering him into his rickshaw. The driver flashes a worth-a-try smile and wiggles his head, in that way, as he leaves. The guy tells me his name is Hemant and I follow him into the hotel.

There are two other young Indian boys working in the reception. I notice a small murti of Ganesh in a large alcove in the wall with a perfumed incense stick smouldering lazily next to it. I sign the register with my details and pay for one night. One of the boys takes me up a few flights of stairs to my room. He unlocks a padlock on the door and slides open the latch to reveal a room with a bed, a table and a ceiling fan. A corner of the room has a tiny doorless bathroom containing a traditional Indian toilet, which is a hole in the floor with raised footsteps on either side. A water tap protrudes knee high from the wall, with a plastic stool and a bucket underneath. No wonder then that these rooms are the price of two bottles of beer per night and popular with backpackers.

I strip off and wash sitting on the plastic stool in the bathroom, throwing water over myself from the bucket. When I finish, I stand dripping wet under the ceiling fan and within minutes I am dry. For the first time today I feel cool and calm like a lake on a windless day.

I hang up the mosquito net over the bed and put my passport, plane ticket, credit card and most of my money in a holster wallet which I lock inside my rucksack. I keep around 800 rupees in my bum bag and I chain and lock the rucksack to the steel bar of the bed. Finally, I spray the whole room with a mosquito and insect killer spray appropriately called HIT. When I get back tonight the room will be mosquito and bug free, and I will crawl under the net into bed. I make sure the door latch is securely padlocked and skip down the stairs. I wave at the boys in reception as I leave the hotel.

The streets are packed with shops and street vendors. There is the same dense humanity and incessant traffic that I have seen in other Indian cities. I find the Old Town and walk through the narrow streets lined with food stalls and bustling with evening trade. A shrug of teenage boys, wearing distinctive school uniforms and holding hands, meander by noisily. They shoo away a mud-stained cow with kumkum and rice splattered on her head that is obstinately in their way. I see an old man sitting on a makeshift wooden skate with uneven wheels on the other side of the road. Both his legs have been cut off above the knee. He stops in front of an air-conditioned shop selling imported western clothes and wails at passers-by pointing his stumpy legs at them. The owner of the shop hurriedly throws a coin into his copper pot and urges him to move on. When I first arrived in India, a sight like this would have moved me to tears.

I buy freshly cooked onion bhajias and eat them whilst I wander around the streets side-stepping the cow pats and ignoring the stares thrown at me. Staring is a very Indian pastime. As evening wears on I make my way to a cafe recommended to me by some backpackers that I'd met in Goa. I find a table and order a cold Kingfisher and before long I start chatting to a couple of Aussies.

'I came here about eight months ago with my girlfriend. But a couple of months later we decided to go our separate ways,' one of them says.

'What happened?' I say with raised eyebrows. He shrugs his shoulders.

'India happened man. Bumped into Greg here a few weeks ago in Goa. How long you done?'

'Three months. Three more to go,' I say.

'You feel like you've come home?' Greg asks.

'Not really,' I say, 'it's tough going. The heat's a killer and nothing works man. Travelling on trains and buses is a real pain.'

'Yep, that's India,' Greg says.

'Might be easier for you than us NRIs.'

'NRIs?'

'Non-resident Indians. I feel like they resent us and try harder to scam us.'

'Resent you for what?' Greg asks.

'Don't know. Getting out of India maybe,' I say. They look puzzled.

'The constant haggling wears me out. I find it difficult to trust them, you know?' There's a pause whilst they digest my words.

'They're just trying to earn a few bucks man,' Greg's mate says.

'India's incredible I reckon. It blows your mind. Got any family here?' Greg says.

'Not really, my parents and most of my relatives are in the UK. I don't think there's any point visiting the villages in Gujarat where they grew up.'

'Might be interesting,' the other Aussie says. 'This is India. Don't ask why, ask why not?'

'Yeah, lighten up man,' Greg says. We laugh and I order more beer.

'Did you come across the ear cleaners in Goa?' I ask.

'Yeah,' Greg laughs, 'but didn't fall for it. You been to Agra yet?'

'Not yet.'

'Watch out for the medical insurance scam.' They fill me in with the details and it's past midnight by the time we finish and say a noisy farewell.

The hotel is in darkness when I get out of the rickshaw. I go up the stairs a little unsteadily holding on to the walls and find my room. I unlock the padlock and pull back the latch and throw open the door. When I switch the light on, the first thing I see is that my mosquito net isn't there. Then I see that my backpack is gone. I stumble into the room realising that all my stuff has gone. My stomach tightens as a sickening nausea grips me. My breathing quickens and then I start to scream as I run down the stairs in darkness to the reception. I can make out the stirring silhouettes of the three boys awakened by my shouting.

'What?' Hemant says.

'All my fucking stuff's gone!'

'Huh?' he says. I grab him by his shirt and shake him.

'Everything is gone,' I scream, 'my rucksack with everything in it, money, passport, tickets... everything. Come on! Come on!'

As we go up the stairs I continue to shout at them.

'Look! I padlocked the fucking door. How could anyone have got in without a key?'

They look at each other in bewilderment.

'You've got another key. You stole my stuff!'

'No...no!' Hemant says. They speak to each other urgently in Hindi.

'You fucking Indians, you're all liars and thieves,' I say. I imagine them sawing through the chain and carrying my rucksack away. I lead them into my room and throw the padlock and keys on the bed in disgust. Even the bug spray which I'd left on the table is gone. One of them leaves whilst the other two stare at me impassively. I sit on the bed, my head in my hands, as I realise the implications of what has happened. I can cancel my credit card but it will take a while to get a temporary passport. The British Embassy in New Delhi is a day and a half away by train. I've been using my passport and credit card to get money out from the banks every month and right now all I have is a few hundred rupees in my bum bag. I'll have to report this to the police though I doubt if I'll ever get my stuff back. The thought of dealing with the Indian police makes my stomach churn.

The third guy returns and mutters something quickly to Hemant.

'Come,' Hemant says, taking my padlock and keys from the bed. As we go up the stairs I wonder if I could cut a deal with them.

'If you give me my stuff back, I'll give you money,' I say, pulling out all the rupees in my bum bag. We stand in front of a room on the next floor up.

'I can give you more money when I get everything back.'

Hemant opens the padlock on the door with my key and swings the door open. The first thing I see is my rucksack chained to the bed and then the mosquito net. I gasp and quickly open the rucksack. My money, passport and tickets are all there. I fall to my knees with relief.

'God, I got the wrong bloody floor! Why did my key unlock the padlock to the room downstairs?' They stare at me silently with smouldering faces. 'I'm sorry,' I say, as they turn away from me and quietly file out of the room.

I hear my mother calling and I turn and walk towards her. As I get closer her face turns into a snarl *'You won't survive in India on your own; You're not Indian, they'll eat you up alive.'* I wake up with a start to the sounds of the city filtering into my room. I stare at the overhead fan whirring away. The events of last night jostle in my mind and I am filled with self-contempt when I think of the things I said to the boys and how I treated them. I get up and make my way downstairs. The three guys are there, red-eyed and drinking tea. I detect a faint trace of sandalwood in the air.

'I'm sorry about last night' I say. Hemant stares at me stony-faced.

'Why did my key unlock the padlock to the room on the floor below?' I ask. His face hardens even more and he turns away busying himself with the mail. I hold out a 100 rupee note. He turns his head, looks at the money and stares coldly at me.

'NRI bastard!' he spits out.

'Well screw you then! I'm not staying another night in this shithole.'

I go back to my room and pack my stuff. The boys have their backs turned towards me when I return to the reception.

'I've paid for one night yeah?' I say, 'you want me to sign out in the register?'

There's no response so I shrug and leave the hotel.

I wave down a rickshaw a few minutes later and climb in. A popular Hindi film song is blaring from a cassette player by the driver's feet. 'Temple?' the driver says. I nod and slump back. A few minutes later I see an Indian family on a Honda Hero motorbike. As my rickshaw passes them, the two youngsters perched in front of their dad, wave at me excitedly. Their mother is holding a baby and sitting side-legged behind her husband. Her nose ring glints in the early morning sunshine. *How can I be Indian and yet I don't feel I belong here in India?* I think of the streets of terraced houses in Leicester where I grew up. Hanging around in the local park with the other kids, going from borrowing books from the library and playing football, to smoking cigarettes behind the library and getting into fights with the white kids who ventured onto our patch. I still remember the anger at finding 'Pakis go home' written in red paint on the library wall. The wasted days in trying to find the perpetrators and in the end just taking revenge mindlessly and getting it returned mindlessly. Images of skinheads with national front banners marching through our area pop into my head. I think of the more subtle unseen prejudices that I learnt were around me later in my working life. I can't honestly say that I've always felt at home in the UK either. Suddenly I burst into tears. The driver glances at me in his mirror as the crying turns into muffled sobbing and pulls off the road to stop in front of a row of chai stalls. He lights a bheedi and holding it within his cupped hands, inhales deeply through a gap between his thumb and index finger.

A boy with short cropped black hair and worn-thin stained shirt and shorts brings two clay pots of chai. He's probably not yet in his teens and is bare-footed. The driver gives him some money and ruffles his hair as he runs back to the stall. I sip the sweet chai and feel calmer.

'Shukriya,' I say. The driver finishes his chai and throws his bheedi away.

'Temple?' he says. I shake my head.

'I think I want to go home,' I say. He looks puzzled.

'Home,' I say again, making a gesture of a flying plane.

'Outside?' he says.

'Yes, outside, I've had enough.'

'No India?'

'No India,' I say.

The driver scratches the stubble on his chin thoughtfully. His oiled black hair showing traces of white on his side parting and sideburns. He has a neatly trimmed salt-and-pepper moustache and the white stubble on his chin stands out on his dark skin. I see a tiny old woman with a bent back and criss-crossing lines etched into her face, shuffle from stall to stall with clasped hands. Each time a seller gives her some food or money, her mouth widens smile-like showing the few decaying teeth she has left, and she touches their heads whispering blessings into their lives.

'Your good name,' the driver says.

'Sanjay,' I say.

'Dharma,' he says touching his chest, 'come.'

'Railway station,' I say.

'Come, come,' he says with a wave of his arm. Dharma drives his rickshaw past a stall selling colourful Ganesh murtis of all sizes and waves at the seller and then drives slowly by another stall. A hand stretches out holding a bulging paper bag. Dharma takes the bag and replaces it with some rupee notes and then dovetails his rickshaw into the stream of mid-day traffic in the full glare of the sun. Every now and then the traffic slows indignantly for people crossing the road but more respectfully for cows sitting on the smoky tarmac chewing nonchalantly.

Soon we are heading out of the city along a highway with fields on either side. Half an hour later Dharma turns his rickshaw off the highway on to a side road and then along a narrow winding dusty path before coming to a stop at a cluster of houses. The houses all have thatched roofs and walls plastered with cow dung. A group of children excitedly crowd around Dharma as he gets out of his rickshaw. He holds a paper bag in the air and drops sweets into their hands, pretend-chastising any child that grabs more than two. He looks over at me and jerks his head.

'Come, come,' he says. I get out and start to strap my rucksack to my back.

'No, no,' Dharma says. I hesitate, not wanting to leave my rucksack but Dharma is striding away holding a child in his arms with three other children trailing behind him.

We walk by fields of sugar cane and past more clusters of houses. We meet more people, and more sweets are handed out to children. We arrive at the side of a small riverbed where several women are sitting cross-legged working and chattering away. They are surrounded by clay murtis of Ganesh. Dharma makes his way to one of the women and he and the children sit around her. I instantly know that this is his family. His wife throws a glance at me and looks at her husband. 'NRI,' Dharma says with a smile at me. I watch the women pressing clay and mud from the riverbed into casts of Ganesh then join the two halves of the casts together. The casts are taken off carefully and the murtis are left to dry in the sun. Some of the women are painting dried murtis of the Remover of all Obstacles in bright colours.

As the day's work ends, everyone takes a finished murti and we make our way back to the village. I see my bags where I'd left them in the rickshaw. That evening we sit cross-legged outside Dharma's home on a blanket. He smokes a bheedi and we watch children playing with sticks and stones. Young men are coming home from their work in the city on motorbikes and on foot from the bus stop on the highway. They all seem to know that I'm a foreigner, but I feel safe here, in a way I haven't felt since I arrived in India. The evening brings with it a cool breeze and I reluctantly think about heading off.

'Railway station,' I say to Dharma.

'Tomorrow, tomorrow' he says. I smile at him and nod. Dharma's eldest daughter brings two thalis of food and places them in front of us. A younger daughter follows with a tower of rotis on a plate and sits down. Soon we are joined by the whole family. The youngest child, a son called Raju, eats from his mother's thali. The food is mildly spiced and the heat is provided by a mango pickle. Dharma pours everyone a spiced watery yoghurt drink from a steel pot and hands me a bottle of Bisleri water.

'One day you live in India?' he says.

'I don't know,' I say. 'I find it difficult here.' Dharma nods thoughtfully.

'Why do people say I'm not Indian? Even my mother says that to me.'

Dharma thinks for a few moments while he chews his food. 'What is Indian? Tamils, Punjabis, Gujaratis, Kashmiris. Hindus, Muslims, Sikhs. Everyone different. This is India,' he says.

After dinner, the men gather and play cards. The women sit close by with their children playing around them. As the light fades paraffin lanterns light up the fronts of the houses. I drink in the simplicity of their lives. This is how my parents must have lived before migrating to the UK. That night I lie on a blanket in the open, lost in the star-studded Indian night sky, listening to the hypnotic sounds of chirping crickets. I think of all the places I'd been to in India and the incredible sights I'd seen. I think of the guy with the stumpy legs begging and the happy faces of the children as they play in the dirt. India is beautiful. India is ugly. A shooting star flares and streaks briefly across the sky before dying. Greg's right, I got to lighten up, I think, as I drift into a deep sleep.

I wake up to the sounds of children playing as they clean their teeth chewing on eucalyptus twigs. Their clothes seem more tattered than I remember from the night before and the cow dung houses smaller. I wave at an old man, who smiles back as he walks by gingerly with stiff joints. Dharma has packed some Ganesh murtis onto a pallet on the roof of his rickshaw secured with ropes and a few inside leaving enough room for me and my bags. I give each of Dharma's kids some money and watch them run gleefully to their mother waving the notes. As we leave there are children running alongside the rickshaw telling Dharma not to forget to bring sweets for them.

Back in the city we stop at the stall selling Ganesh murtis and I help Dharma unload the murtis from his rickshaw. The boy brings us two pots of chai and I give him money and ruffle his hair. We finish our chai and Dharma says 'railway station?'

'Yes,' I say 'but take me to Hotel Shalimar first.'

Hemant looks surprised when I place the murti on the counter, as do the other two boys behind him. One of the boys takes the old murti out of the alcove and replaces it with my gift. The brightly coloured Ganesh fits in the alcove snugly. Hemant, still stony-faced, gives me a nod as I turn and leave.

'Railway station Dharma,' I say getting into the waiting rickshaw.

'Going outside?' Dharma asks making the gesture of a plane flying, 'home?'

'Not yet,' I say. 'I think I'd like to see the villages where my parents grew up.'

'Why not?' says Dharma wiggling his head in that way.

Alan Beard

Alan Beard has published two story collections: *Taking Doreen Out of the Sky* (Picador, 1999) and *You Don't Have to Say* (Tindal Street Press, 2010). He has had numerous stories and flashes in magazines and anthologies, in the UK, USA and Canada including Malahat Review, London Magazine, Warwick Review, Critical Quarterly, *Best British Short Stories* (Salt), and most recently, *Digbeth Stories* (Floodgate, 2023). He has also had several stories broadcast on Radio 4. He won the Tom Gallon award for best short story, and was longlisted for the Edge Hill and Bridport prizes. He has been a member of TSFG since 1985 and is grateful for the group's critical input and encouragement over the years. Indeed TSFG published his first collection '...Doreen...' in 1997 as a dry run for the setting up of Tindal Street Press. It proved very successful, gaining many positive reviews, and resulted in Picador re-publishing the collection in 1999. He is currently finishing off a third collection.

Had a husband once, for a year and a day, but no child, although I pretend I do have one, a boy, now and then. Craig, my craggy Craig about eight then again ten depending on who I'm with—must keep track—anyway always a little boy to tell them about, neighbours and pals, a boy I play football with on the beach, though there's no beach. I'm quite good at football, I know the names of footballers, watch it now and then—cup finals and things—and the boy would have a 'mop of hair' I would ruffle and comb and remark on in the mornings when we had our breakfast and I asked him about schoolwork. Now of course home-school work, downloading lessons and whatnot.

The gone husband? Practised the niceties, touch of religion in him like a slim line running through his body ending in the little tail peeping out. Like Harry after him he picked me up at work, or I him, I forget, but unlike H. went through all the hoo-ha of a divorce to marry me. But I think he missed the guilt, the delicious guilt, for him a would-be man of the cloth. Yes, a wannabe vicar. Flirted with it, he said (flirted with everything, I said), felt a calling in my youth and applied to *theological* college. He liked that word. How could he be a vicar, his hands all over women and the world, what little of it he got offered, his fingerprints of grease and want, his speech fouling up perfectly good air. It's a twisty, cunting road you put us on, oh Lord, you deal out your hands unevenly: him in his wanky prayers every night.

His guilt like pillows and clouds reclined on, but he also ranted and stamped his foot. He thought he was endearing and lovable, his mother encouraging him, standing by his side on visits and simpering.

He was a box ticker, out walking he'd see an old fort, the ruins of a monastery with always the joke about my face, nod at it, tick it off mentally, and walk on. 'Got the T-shirt' a favourite phrase of his, along with 'to be fair'—he had a strange idea of fair. Womanising was fair, in that it was *natural.*

He got rid of the microwave, heard it gave you cancer but continued to smoke until recently—I hear now he vapes. I was a box ticked off, took little more than a year to get to the bottom of me. Now I am a divorcee, I am a spinster like my aunt was. She would be on at me about my slovenliness, my manners, the way I'm bringing up Craig. She appears in my dreams now, brushing my hair obsessively, until it gleams and more, until my eyes fall out.

He could be kicky, he would leave you in a service station in a faraway town built in the 80s or in a coronavirus hotspot on a Sunday if there had been coronavirus around in those days; he could be tie wearing and corduroy and desert boot, kind looking, wispy but behind closed doors in his car on the corner of roads or in the back of some out of town Cotswold stone bar, some midday bar he could be sharp, grip you, the hissing tongue of him slipping around. That sharpness that pout and the silence in the mornings was just like my mother's ex before he died, before they both died: do we marry a type? Wonder what he'll be up to now seeking out some vicarry truth with his new woman or practising some bon mot some one liner to give out to the neighbour tomorrow as he wishes them good day the breath of him rancid.

Two or so years after hubby was Harry and he worked right up the corridor and took his turn in my queue at lunchtime. I was always Harry's as soon as he arrived and trained us in things we already knew.

Just before lockdown the girls got together for a reunion and never told me, back in the area and making myself known. That was a mistake because I'm going to gate crash the next one and go round and remind them of their misdemeanours loudly in the chosen pub, packets of crisps ripped open to be shared on the tables, rolls and sausage rolls and rolls of sound about the past and what it was like for them which teacher lost control who set fire to their hair in Chemistry who wrote what on the board, the class bully the class victims still in the seating arrangements. Evelyn the organiser (I learn from Facebook) has got bustier and reddened her hair in line with her husband and child. I met her somewhere on the school run I forget where and she told me not to call her Eve any more, nobody did any more.

School to me a long damp corridor, squatting grey and red brick buildings amongst sparse trees; dark headed bald headed bewigged teachers spouting, the road to revolution, the inner logic of atoms. Three blind mice. Disintegration of interest was rapid, felt it crumble crumble inside.

A dinner maybe a dance do they still have dinner and dances? Do they still play darts? The football machine we all played do you remember that in the sixth form, the games of bridge, never played it since I will say. Oh I have, Evelyn, bosomy and nurturing, will say, I play it all the time and there are fortnightly schools round my house if you want to come, new packs each time, bring a nice bottle of wine. That's how it would go, and I would get in with that crowd, the bridge playing, sports car brigade and maybe for some weeks they'd let me in, and speak of their gardens and lovers and spa days, while they swapped cards about in their hands, the days ahead, the days forgotten, but one day one night with drink consumed, the Labrador on the rug behind us in the room with spot lit framed prints of holiday views on the walls, they'd say I ruined it with my questions and peculiar smell.

There were men before and between husband number one— I'm optimistic—who I called Oswald though his name was Neville, and Harry, my dark-haired Harry who was, is, with his even features and clear eyes his voice like something humming, a cleaned-up version of Oswald, my husband put through the wash, a bolder smoother version, one with all his worries and twitches ironed out.

Other men went by and by. The best of them out of reach, frying their own fish, their own books to read, programmes to watch, hobbies to maintain and laughs to laugh with someone else. The one with McCartney's accent but who couldn't sing. The one who always talked of our 'love' when there wasn't any, little. The hairs in this one's nose and ears, his views on the Arab spring and his skunky genitals and premiership football obsession: he moved in for a while, measured our weeks by matches and then left at the end of the season.

Cold cold ones who wanted stuff from you, sex, a play made from it, a particular two scene act over and over again and got you to dress like this or like that maybe it's their mother fantasies or a girl seen when they were adolescent forming ideas about who women were, what they were like. One told me men—all?—are after reliving a moment over and over and fixated a lot of them on first loves or aunties or cousins seen first in the nude or half nude at someone's paddling pool party with younger kids about giving it a soundtrack of wellbeing, pretend screams and hide and seek and splashes, water droplets on skin, sunlight. I never had that, siblings, afternoons splashing in the garden.

Imagine if I'd stayed with this or that 'boyfriend'. Stalk them on Facebook with their wives their trips to the zoo and getting the sled out in winter. Men on a merry go round in my head, the dropping off points. Harry never online and now we're all working from home I never see him except in glimpses when I drive to his street and park opposite to watch him and his wife walk by and take in her size and gait next to him, see how they fit together, the places they touch, elbow and hip, kids running behind and before making bombing noises, chuckling and singing, three mites: I know the order of them, gender, age, but not what they smell like. He never looks over to see my best side.

Imagine all the kids I could have had, not just one, how they would grow up I could tell them secrets I could lead them astray I could sing them a song I could follow them around I would go to their dens I would ruin their lives.

COVID did for us. I'd see him at work even after he'd made me delete his flirty titbit emails, stood over me, pretending to help sort out my software, hissing like a slow puncture at me. Bit macho, I said, as he got me to empty the trash folder too, when are you due? The end he kept saying, the end got it? No following around no pissing about no eye widening, no big welcome when I come in or that movement of your knee, don't think I haven't noticed. I'm losing patience losing the will to live losing my temper now get on with it don't ring me don't message me don't look at me. Fucker, should have spat in his soup so to speak, snapped off his cock and presented it to his wife, instead the usual crying in the back of his car round the corner from his family watching Disney plus or gaming or social messaging on their devices, our phones turned off, Sunday sex or something like, a pulling of this, a smudging of that, some squirming about. Unsatisfactory, but I would have put up with it. I'd see him in the corridor, in the canteen, remembering our assignations in smaller and smaller hotels increasingly out of town, making our way up badly carpeted stairs. He only came back to my house once, said he could feel my aunt watching us, wouldn't come again.

After sex we'd sprawl together and discuss books. Well, I'd listen, his voice purring. Harry is a reader, the latest Booker winner, stuff like that. He said Marlon James was difficult, full of Jamaican patois, inside violent gangsters' heads, but it was worth it for the Bob Marley bits. (I sang Three Little Birds in the shower once). He got me reading novels again, all the way through, not the Seven Killings, but Austen, the Brontes, Hardy, stuff I read at school. With our love of different eras and genres we complemented each other. I said this to him, I said we'd make an ideal couple, and he agreed. He agreed.

He was going to run away with me to Mexico to France to Wales we were going to live up a mountainside with a view of the sea and catch rabbits or something or in a caravan by the side of a road or get jobs in a bar and be live-in staff in a little room with a sink and a black and white telly. Do they still have black and white tellies?

I told him I wouldn't mind if his kids visited, Christ they could even live with us (eventually). They could play in the back yard: I wouldn't trip them up. I would support, not like my aunt who never listened. I would cock my ear—I would be a proper mum, hug them, warn them of predators, introduce them to Craig. They would all get along. We'd be a chuckling family unit sweeping into restaurants and theme parks, joshing each other. People would look.

You know how sometimes people look wrongly together, their heads/faces not right for their bodies, their legs belong to someone else? Well, Harry fit together perfectly. He was all of a piece. He was a warm feeling like a drug that worked. Until he turned away, basically a coward with hair on his knuckles. Now with working from home I never see him going past my desk trying to avoid my eyes and me saying 'Hi Harry, how's the kids?' and him forced to look at me and saying fine. He even seems to avoid the zoom meetings we should be in together where maybe I could examine him, look for lines on that face, look for a wink in the little square he occupied but his head and shoulders never turn up.

Craig's growing up quickly going to secondary next term, now schools are re-opening, same one as I went to, St B.'s, naturally, he's not getting away with not being fucked up for life like the rest of us.

Indoors we play – the task of finding him over and over beneath curtains and round doors, he hid in a bin once I could have killed him the fright he gave me. We sing into broomsticks and hair dryers when I can get the little bugger off the sofa, he'll reluctantly sing Rihanna—Diamonds—when I can unglue him from his World of Warcraft game. 'Screentime!' I admonish him, pointing to my non-existent watch. I'm a good mum, I protect him from bullies, I pursue his case down the school I wasn't letting the sourpuss Head have her way with my boy.

I scrimped and saved to bring him up properly, weaned him off his dad, Jesus botherer Oswald. Luckily he doesn't resemble him. We're settled now at my aunt's old house, a slab of terrace, with the wind pressing front and back. My aunt brought me up here from 8 onwards. Hardly noticing me, except to pinch and complain about my noise, preoccupied I thought, but what it was was Pick's disease setting in.

Harry moving on, or moving back to the skinny wife's arms. I was on the ball once, but deteriorating at a rate now, when I'm only 36 or 39 or 42.

Next door's music streaming, Alexa-ed into their rooms. Noisy bunch, now getting an extension until the pandemic stopped it. They used to have outdoors do's, laughter coming over with the smoke of barbecues, friends and family I presume standing on grass in heels with glasses of prosecco you swirl by the stem, nothing like that for them or anyone these days as we all sit in our houses unable to get out, *except for essentials.*

Everybody's in, all down the street, invisible crowds all about. Children, adults, dogs all stuffed next door both ways every hour of the day. Working from home like me—they can't do without me, without me information doesn't get distributed—or home schooling or lazing playing computer games like Craig always upstairs. In the evenings I watch Scandi-noir, it all looks so easy, hand-cuffed to a radiator.

I was going to be a new me, weren't we all once restrictions had been lifted and we could go running again. I had in mind long miles down the towpath and across parks only inadvertently showing up in his street again. I would join a running club. I bought all the gear, had it delivered but only tried it on once. Not my style. Leave that sort of thing to Evelyn or Harry's wife (Anna, Elaine—as if I didn't know). Instead I tried on dresses I hadn't put on since the divorce and I went on a few Tinder dates, black showing a little bosom when I leant over the steak and wine. They were all disappointing, Oswald-a-likes—is it me? Although with one suitably dark haired, stubbled, I stayed out all night by the canal drinking whisky out of a bottle. You're as fucked up as me, he said.

With the schools re-opened I bump into Evelyn and her cronies more and more on this corner or that, on their way to school or back.

Now for instance by the shops a group of them, assorted mates fresh from devouring each other's gossip last night when they played bridge and got mildly pissed. One with a dog, a blue grey greyhound thing on a lead, a pushchair or two. Empty trains go by over the bridge behind them. Evelyn says there should only be gatherings of six outside and I would make it seven. Only if you count the kids, I say. And I go round and look into the faces of these chewing, crying, uncaring toddlers, although one is smiling and it stops me, someone smiling at me. Lovely, lovely, they're all lovely, I say. I beam.

'Craig,' I say, straightening up, 'do you know the name stands for a mischievous and open person? I looked it up. "A Craig is always athletic, hardworking and many ladies view him as handsome."'

I never let myself stink, I say to the group of mumble sharers who hate me, it's there in their pleated mouths and skirts, I take a shower at least three times a day. They lift their eyes to me temporarily to take in my cleanliness.

I offer my services, as humble as you like, I've read my Dickens, I say I'll pick up Adrian along with my Craig when he starts back, when he gets out of hospital because now he's gone and got the 'rona on top of all his usual problems. Complications. His lungs all sticky with it, like he's been smoking all his eleven years, I say, it was like someone else speaking. They stand the mandatory six feet away or so, black, blue, spotted, leopard skin masks tucked under their chins. Evelyn has a charity badge on her jumper. I think she's about to ask for money, sponsorship, but she is saying first time she let her Adrian walk home alone was heart stopping. She lightly thumps her breast.

'I let Craig do his own thing,' I tell her, 'room of his own to do whatever in. Don't go in there, just lean against the door now and then, strain to hear, but he's not noisy, you know, sadly, I'd like to hear some hip hop blasting out.'

'You can have mine for a night,' Evelyn laughs through her top front teeth. 'Do a swap.' Her Adrian she's offering me and I know he bullies Craig. Her Adrian who might become a banker like his dad, she'd said before on another corner, he's got that type of brain, bashed Craig nightly when he was about, when the time was ripe. Her son rangy and gloopy and not a patch on my compact kid even if hers is growing a scattered gingery moustache. Craig told me, back from school as the Chase was on when he should be doing his homework learning about kings and queens and reading novels. 1984 and Catch 22. He told me the ginger lad's reach was too long. He told me gloomily how Adrian led a small gang determined to humiliate him in lessons, it was Craig sir, craggy Craig, and playtime, constantly coming up and sniping, pinching and pulling and snapping little bits off my son, football star of the future, the one who'll support me in old age, will maybe watch me shrivel and burn like my aunt, who'll get me things from the shop. They gouge out little bits of him and take them away and throw them in drains and bramble until there is nothing left.

"'I'm telling you honey," I say to him,' I say to them ranged across the shopfront pavement in their Ugg boots and mittens, 'you've got to straighten up if you want to play for Villa.'

So it was pick up the kid, the third, the easiest, with his flipfloppy hair and his Harry eyes, snatch him from the street, drive past and bundle him headfirst into the boot hurting Harry where it hurts most, he told me he was his favourite, the way he got lyrics wrong in songs, said diso-naur. Really show him; could hide Junior in the basement, I'd go down and taunt him about his blue eyes and his butter-and-stale-biscuit smell, get him to sing a wrong lyrics song, except I haven't got a basement, in the attic then the bathroom except workmen have come back to populate the scaffolding next door. Workmen drilling drilling at all levels, glimpses of work boots and calves even though it's not sunny, shorts mandatory, tools stuffed here and there they look as if they're about to enter through the window. So no couldn't bring him here, even though I could then parade him about down the shops, in front of the gathering, ruffle his hair and say look here's Craig, not exactly as described, younger, a fair bit younger, the famous Craig who can do 50 keepie-uppies can't you Craig, watched by Villa scouts on windy touchlines. Under my hand wholly, no thanks are due to his father, doesn't he look like me got my upturned nose and serene nature. When he's a footballer, a midfield dynamo, earning their and their husbands' annual salaries combined in a day, in an hour, the bridge players would let me in would be amazed at my progress how quickly I'd become an expert, trump them, I was always the one that was missing in their lives, the vaping lot of them, the piece that made them whole.

The disease took away many of my aunt's functions, speech, movement, digestion, and she had to go live in a nursing home. I took a train to visit now and then. Her eyes did lock on mine but otherwise nothing much. She used to hum along to songs, nursery rhymes, Grand Old Duke of York but even that went. Instead I had one-sided conversations about her atrocious parenting skills and how ill equipped she'd left me. How we never went on holiday, and I used to watch the other families pack their cars and disappear in the summer and return burned and happy playing some new game they'd learned in the street. The elderly nurse would come to spoon-feed her sludge which she sometimes swallowed, talking to her and to me as if she understood. To get the food down the nurse had to massage her neck.

Her whole body thinned out, breastless, curled up, hands claws. Unmoving, clenched. I told her what she'd been like in those last few months at home, how she stood next to radiators until she burnt, how she gave all her money to toddlers in supermarkets and chased them down the aisles, as if now she liked children, how she began to wet herself. Her only response was a slow movement of the head. Other residents in the room ignored her except tall bald Eric who shut all the windows 'to keep the bairns out' and came and stood close to her chair and half took off his jumper.

Harry—at work—gave a little lurch towards me—couldn't help himself he always said—when he came through the door.

I wasn't stalking him, your honour.

He could teach me things, besides which books to read, there are things I don't know and need to. So many things, he could teach me politics, religion, laugh with me about my vicar husband, show me with his fingers and elbow back how to skim stones, he could teach Craig to swim.

He didn't know what was happening to him, he said, but he couldn't leave me alone, especially after the family fortnight abroad (Spain): he was at me, exuding waves of heat picked up and stored in his skin, almost indiscreet, snatching moments while the big fan whirred, while IT repaired our computers. I knew at lunch we'd be in his car. The afternoon meetings our thighs pressed together under the table – look no hands – turn up late or not turn up at all.

Tell her what he called her behind her back, the spit at his lips, the comfort I gave him that he took and took.

He praised my beauty my slimness my legs my spine even. My imagination when I haven't any. My smile, my smell. Want to hear his voice again, the small humming machine of it.

When I go to beat Adrian how shall I dress? What would be best to wear for ripping him to shreds, rip him to little crawling pieces, his skin and bones like insects running off? To pay back the fear he's put in my poor Craig reduced to a whimpering blob in his bedroom not the sort of noise I want to hear from his door. After bullying him on social media: a WhatsApp group, Instagram, TikTok, things became real, things escalated. Craig returning in tears, I'm telling you, snotty, hair sweaty, some gunk in it, he didn't want to tell, but I got it out of him. Adrian using him as a punchbag, showing off to his mates, Craig shorter, hopeless. He is disappearing but doesn't want me to make a fuss. I see, I say, I understand, but, I tell him, setting my jaw, enough is enough. So, what would be best? You know I take my date dress down, don't you? You know I do my make up even more carefully, thinking of the later mugshots that might appear. How my unsmiling face and profile will blow up twitter.

I've done the legwork, followed him, see the Evelyn in him: the stance, the gait, but the dad too, see which way he goes home which bit of urban brook he passes, maybe push him in, which I'm sure he did to Craig, although Craig says no, mum, I fell in. I've planned it out. The corner where he parts from his mates, where he can be tackled the large hedge hiding the business, the punch I will deliver and have practised on pillows propped on the sofa. Maybe with a fistful of keys.

I'll drag him by his ears as in those comics we read in the moonlight of our scruffy childhoods, hiding from our aunts who didn't like us reading. Here he is coming round that corner in his tall sandy world, knees that have dead legged Craig in dinner queues, sniffing to himself to hear the sound it makes on the apparently empty afternoon street. I will confront the lanky devil, I'll be fair though, I'll explain it may not be his fault with a mother like that before I hit him and hit him again.

Polly Wright

Polly Wright is a theatre director, occasional performer, facilitator, writer, lecturer, and researcher. She co-founded Women and Theatre in Birmingham, where she co-wrote and performed in many cabaret sketches and plays. She is the artistic director of the Hearth Centre, which is a centre for Health, Education and the Humanities with Art at the Heart, for which she has been the sole playwright of eight plays, all of which have been professionally produced.
Website: www.thehearthcentre.org.uk

She has published six short stories and five poems in various anthologies (including Tindal Street and Diva Presses), in addition to being a sole and co-author of five academic articles/chapters.

About six years ago, when sorting through her late grandmother's effects, Polly discovered some letters from an Italian Prisoner of War after he had been placed on her grandparents' farm in Wales during World War Two. Polly wrote a play called *Friends of Enemies* about the subject, for which she received Arts Council development money to support a short tour. Lockdown prevented plans for a full production, so she worked on the material to adapt it into a short story, which is included in this anthology. She is now working on a novel of the same name.

Swallows! The flash of ink wings and a glimpse of rust throats. Swooping and dipping, swivelling, and diving, the male in front of the female. No dithering. Knowing exactly where they were going. To Pen Y Bryn, the farm in the lea of Moel Famau. She would tell Mario when she got back. *Le rondini sono qui.* A sign that spring is truly on its way. They'll come to our farm very soon, she'd say. And will nest in the granary where you're sleeping.

The Commander had offered her a lift from the Italian Prisoner of War camp to the police station, after their 'post mortem', as he called it, about the concert. Elizabeth had thanked him, saying she'd prefer to walk on such a beautiful day and admire the gardens on the edge of the little town. Yellow and white are the colours of our spring in this country, she'd say to Mario. Is that the same in yours? White cherry blossom – well you can get pink but white's the best of all. *Loveliest of trees, the cherry now/Is hung with bloom along the bough* she'd quote. She couldn't quite remember the middle bit, she'd look it up in the *Golden Treasury*, but she remembered the last line of the first verse: *And wearing white for Eastertide.* And yellow daffodils, no, *golden* daffodils, of course. She asked him yesterday if they had daffodils in Italy – and he had said they were called narcissi. She'd replied that there were flowers called narcissi, but they were smaller and paler than daffodils – but at that point Dai had come into the kitchen and spoilt it.

'You're not going on again about bloody crowds of daffodils, are you?' he'd said and she felt hurt.

'I'm surprised at you,' she said. 'Swearing about your national flower.' When they'd first got engaged, they'd copied out poems they had learnt at school and sent them to each other. She'd copied out Wordsworth and he'd copied poems by a Welsh poet who'd died in the first war, Hedd Wyn, with a translation to help her learn Welsh. But after they'd got married all that had gone out of the window.

Elizabeth turned her thoughts away from her husband to the concert at POW camp the night before. The Commander said she should feel proud of herself for such a resounding success, because really it had been all her brainchild. She had said that wasn't true – it had been his idea. But, in truth, she did feel proud. Proud of Mario's face as he'd turned to her, when they had all stamped and applauded, his compatriots. Proud that even the squaddies had clapped, though they probably preferred the comedy routine. Mario had had tears in his eyes – though, of course, that didn't mean much. Italians cried at anything, as everyone said.

Crossing the bridge, which was the town's boundary, she saw Tomas Hamblas, the telegraph boy, wheeling his bike on the other side of the road. She stopped in her tracks. It *was* him – she had been sure she saw him last night. Dressed up in a POW uniform which was too tight for him. He was right at the back, but her eyesight was good and she would recognise his podgy face anywhere. She'd known him since he was a child when she used to give him piano lessons.

'Tommy!' she shouted and waved, but it seemed he didn't hear her. She shouted again, 'Tommeee!' But then a tractor and trailer rattled between them (Government issue, she noted), and when they had passed, Tommy had disappeared.

Perhaps he hadn't wanted to see her? She suspected that impersonating a Prisoner of War was against the law. And she'd have been the only person who'd have known who he was. But she wouldn't report him. She was glad that her former pupil loved music so much that he'd risk breaking the law. And it was funny, too, seeing him there. Pink-faced, with all those swarthy Italians. Like a piglet, squashed in with a lot of wolves.

She looked at her watch and realised she needed to hurry up if she wasn't going to be late for PC Jones. She wasn't particularly concerned about being called to the police station; she knew what it was going to be about – hidden pigs in the hill farms again. Another thing she'd have to shout at Dai about when she got home.

'*You're* the Welsh speaker. The farmers listen to you!'

But when she got to the station there didn't seem to be anybody about. So much for punctuality, she thought. She sat in the cold foyer and read the notices about blackouts and the need to declare all your livestock. What a stupid place to put them, she thought. As if the real culprits are ever here!

Not unless they'd been arrested. And then it'd be closing the barn door.

'Thank you for coming in, Mrs Williams.' PC Jones was behind her.

She had been expecting him to come through a different door, the one behind the counter. 'Geraint!' she said. 'You gave me a shock.'

'I'm sorry about that, Mrs Williams.'

'Is it about the pig at Bryn Glas? I'm sorry, that man was lying through his teeth. Dai's going up there today...'

'We're in here, today, Mrs Williams,' he interrupted. He held the door of the Chief Inspector's office open for her.

'Have you been promoted, Geraint?' She expected him to laugh.

But he just pulled a chair out for her and said, 'Chief Inspector Evans will be with you in a moment.'

'Oh,' she said, adjusting her voice to match the coldness of his. 'Not too long, I hope. I have to be back to get the lunch ready for the men.' And to see Mario, she added in her head. She couldn't wait to re-live the evening's concert with him. And tell him what Commander Matthews had said. 'Such a fine tenor, Mrs Williams. Perhaps we can call upon his services again?'

'Would you like a cup of tea, Mrs Williams?'

'No thank you, Geraint. As I said, I need to get back to the farm.'

The door shut behind the constable and she was left in a room which was as cheerless as a prison cell.

It was strange that the Chief Inspector wanted to see her. All her dealings up to now had been with the War Reserve PCs, Geraint and Ioan. Perhaps there'd been some directive from the top about black market activity. If so, that was Dai's department, wasn't it? He was the Chair of the War Ag., after all.

After a few minutes of waiting, she clicked open her handbag and got out her powder compact.

'Mrs Williams.'

'Oh, hello. I'm sorry. I didn't hear you...' She jumped up and put out her right hand to shake his, all at the same time, so the powder compact dropped on the floor.

'Allow me,' the Chief Inspector said, picking it up and handing it back to her. 'I do hope it isn't broken. My wife says those things are quite expensive.'

'No, no. It's fine,' she replied, shoving it back in her bag roughly to cover her embarrassment.

But as he sat down behind the desk opposite her, she cried. 'Osian! Osian Evans!'

'At your service,' he replied with a slight nod.

'I didn't know they'd made you Chief Inspector. Well done!' He looked away, catching her patronising tone. 'When did that happen?'

'You must have heard of the last Chief Inspector's heart attack?'

'Oh yes. But Dai, my husband, told me he'd recovered.'

'Happily, yes. But he can't work again, so I was the obvious choice, I suppose. Younger candidates all called up, of course.'

'I'm sure that wasn't the reason,' she said politely, though it had crossed her mind that it was.

'And how are you, Mrs Williams?' he said, taking the top off his fountain pen. 'All going well up at Caer Eithin?' He opened the top drawer of the desk and took out an official-looking form.

'Oh yes, very well. You know they've placed prisoners with us now? Italians. They're a rowdy lot, but they work hard. Well, some of them do.'

She looked at the strands of hair stretched over the top of his head as he bent over the form and wondered how old he was now. Fifty-five, perhaps? He seemed quite old back when she first met him, when she'd moved to Wales to marry Dai, and she had the idea he was, maybe, a little bit sweet on her. He'd been a farmer himself, then, but the family farm had gone bust, like many after the First World War, so he'd gone into the police force.

'Right,' he said. 'Mrs Williams.'

'Elizabeth, please.'

The Chief inspector coughed. 'Er, Elizabeth. Could you do me a favour, please? Sign this, er, form.' He turned the paper round.

'A form?'

'For our records. Formality, really. Whenever we talk to anybody. Do you have a pen?'

'Just a sec.' She fumbled in her handbag again, and pulled out her pen, which, to her irritation, was brushed with powder from the compact, which *had* broken. She signed the paper.

'Thank you, Mrs Williams. You must be wondering.'

'Well, yes, Osian, to be honest, I was. If it's about the black market, then I've done all I can. It's Dai you need to talk to. He's the one who should be getting the *intelligence,* if you like.'

'I suppose it's difficult for you to get up to Bryn Glas and Bryn Mawr.'

'I'm perfectly capable of getting up there in the tractor, though it was well-nigh impossible – for anybody – last winter, in the snow. No, I'm talking about Dai's Welsh, of course, Osian. He can see through any of their...'

'Lies?'

'Stories, I was going to say.'

The Inspector smiled and went on. 'So how has the Welsh been going, Mrs Williams? I remember you were learning.' He had the sort of watery blue eyes which are too pale, making the owner seem vulnerable. Not an ideal feature for a policeman, she thought.

'Oh well, you know. It's been rather side-lined. By the Italian.' She smiled.

'The Italian,' he said. 'Of course.'

'Italian's easier. Even if my Welsh was a little better, they could still pull the wool. The farmers, that is.'

'Of course,' he said. 'An appropriate metaphor when dealing with sheep farmers.' He smiled. 'You were saying. About the Italian POWs?'

'Oh yes. They are rowdy and they can be argumentative, but they're great fun.'

'And you speak to them in their own language?'

'Yes. The Sergeant from the camp gave us a dictionary, but it's pretty basic. I learnt a bit of Italian at school, so I got out my old grammar and I try to read it every night – and, of course, I have the opportunity for conversation every day. Mario says...'

'Mario?'

'Mario. One of the POWs. He's not very strong, physically, so we decided that he would help me in the kitchen. We talk all the time. He says he can't believe how good my accent is. The other day he said I could be mistaken for someone from Milan. But I'm sure he's just saying that.'

'Would that be Mario Golinelli?'

'Golinelli, yes.'

'Golinelli,' he repeated.

'Yes.' Elizabeth gave a little laugh. 'Though you have to stress the penultimate syllable – Goli*nell*i.' She broke off when the Chief Inspector scraped back his chair and went to the door. He shouted something in Welsh to Geraint, who arrived so quickly she thought he must have been listening outside. He handed the Chief Inspector an air mail letter which he put on the table in front of Elizabeth.

'Golinelli. As in Signora Golinelli?' he said.

They both looked at it in silence.

Eventually she said, 'Where did Geraint...?'

'That is your handwriting, isn't it?' The Inspector pointed at the address section, and then to her signature on the form. She felt herself go hot and put her hand to her face.

He went back to his side of the desk and read: 'Signora Golinelli, Castelluccio, Modena. Forgive me, Mrs Williams. My geography isn't very good. Can you tell me exactly where that is in Italy?'

'Near Bologna,' she replied.

'Bologna.'

'Yes.'

'A beautiful, ancient city, perhaps?'

'I haven't been there. But yes, I believe it is beautiful.'

'In Northern Italy?'

'Yes.'

'Occupied territory.'

Elizabeth said nothing but looked down at her hands.

'I couldn't find Castelluccio on the map,' the Chief Inspector went on.

'It's too small,' she replied. 'It's a bit confusing. There's another one in Umbria. When we looked for it...'

'We?' said the Chief Inspector.

' Me and Mar...'

'Mario Golin*ell*i?' Was it her imagination, or was his emphasis on the last syllable of Mario's surname sarcastic? 'Our intelligence is that Castelluccio is very close to the line.'

'What line?'

'The one between Allied and occupied territory. You knew that, presumably?'

'No!' she exclaimed. 'No, I didn't.'

'You read the papers, don't you? Intelligent woman like you, Mrs Williams.'

'But not... not in that sort of detail.'

'Really?' The inspector paused. 'We took the liberty of opening the letter, as required by the Government for all letters to foreign destinations.' Suddenly the Chief Inspector seemed to be playing a part in a play. He unfolded the flimsy paper with a slight flourish, as if it was a prop. 'Could you translate it for me?'

'Oh no, I couldn't.'

'You've just told me,' he said, 'that you speak Italian like a native?'

'No, I said Mario said my accent's like a native.'

'Same difference.' He paused before adding, 'Mario again. I'm assuming Signora Golinelli is his mother?'

She nodded, winding the corner of her handkerchief round her little finger.

'So, *you* wrote the letter, didn't you?'

'No, of course I didn't. It's from a son to his mother.'

The Chief Inspector spoke more gently. 'It's very short. If you could oblige, Elizabeth?'

She took the letter slowly and translated aloud, '*My Dear Mother, I hope this letter finds you well. I'm sure you know that I was taken prisoner in Libya, but I am writing to let you know I am safe and being well looked after in Wales. Your most affectionate and devoted son, Mario.*'

There was a pause, during which Elizabeth noticed a spider's web in the corner of the room, its silver triangles glistening in a shaft of sun.

'I hear it was Mario Gollinelli who sang at the Pool Park concert last night. With you? Aren't I right?'

'How did you know?'

'Commander Matthews told me. You were responsible for planning the whole event, he said.'

She shook her head. 'Not really, no.'

It seemed to her that the Chief Inspector's watery eyes had narrowed and lost their vulnerability. He coughed, picked up the letter again and read: '*Sicuro e bene e essere curato in Galles?* Safe and being looked after in Wales?'

'Yes,' she said.

'And do you write to all their mothers? Or only the ones in Northern Italy?' After a pause, he went on, 'The POWs from Southern Italy are allowed to post their own letters home, aren't they? Now we're on the same side. You do know the difference, don't you?'

'*Of course* I do, Osian! I just...' *Oh God, I'm going to cry*, she thought and fumbled in her bag for her handkerchief. 'It's just that... wherever they come from, I understand how desperately the POWs want their families to know that... they're all right. I would want Christopher... I mean, wouldn't you, Osian? Your son? Let you know how he was? If he was away at war?' She blew her nose hard. 'I'm sorry.'

The Chief Inspector's tone changed. 'Don't upset yourself.' He waited until she had finished, and said, quietly, 'Elizabeth, we know that Mario wrote the letter himself. Just one look at the handwriting tells us that. But what is a bit strange, is that you addressed the letter for him?' He sighed.

'As I said before, you're an intelligent woman. You must have known that enemy POWs can't send letters home of their own volition. Which is why the address is in your handwriting? Not to put too fine a point on it, Elizabeth, you wanted the Post Office to think that the letter was from you.' She screwed her handkerchief into a ball. 'Perhaps the Welsh farmers aren't the only people pulling the wool?'

Elizabeth used the handkerchief to cover her eyes, hiding the tears.

He coughed. 'Does Mr Williams, Dai, know about this? About you writing to this POW's mother? In occupied territory?'

She shook her head.

'As the Chair of the Agricultural Committee, he ought to know that his wife has committed an act of, well, subterfuge. Some might even say treachery,'

'*Treachery?*'

'Well, not quite treachery. Have you heard of *fraternisation*, Mrs Williams?' Receiving no answer, he went on, 'Some women in London have been fined.'

'What for?' Her voice was shaky.

'Writing letters.'

'To whom?'

'POWs. Or *for* POWs.'

'Fined? How much?'

'One pound, I understand. But Mrs Williams, surely, it isn't the amount that matters? There would be a court case.'

'Court case?''

'Why didn't you tell your husband, Elizabeth? Why didn't you just say, "Mario wants to write to his mother. Shall we talk to Commander Matthews about it?"'

'Don't,' Elizabeth pleaded. 'Don't tell Dai. Osian. Please.'

He started to reply when he was interrupted by the noise of a plane overhead which made them both look up. The Chief Inspector walked to the back wall to peer at the rectangle of sky.

'One of ours. On their way back to Wrexham,' he said, and went to the door to call, 'Geraint. A glass of water for Mrs Williams please,' before resuming his post at the high window. Neither he nor Elizabeth spoke until Geraint came back with a cup without its saucer.

'Thanks, Geraint,' she said, as she drank the lukewarm water.

'Ah. Swallows,' the Chief Inspector said, still with his back to her. 'First sign of summer.'

'Spring,' Elizabeth said automatically.

'Same difference,' he said with a smile.

The day was just as beautiful as it had been in the morning, but when she left the police station, on her way back to the farm, it no longer felt fresh. Instead, the spring warmth was almost oppressive as she trudged along in her coat and heavy winter shoes. It was a long walk back to the farm. She wished now that she'd taken the tractor to go to the camp, as Dai had suggested that morning.

Foolish, Osian had said. Of course, it had been very *foolish*. She could feel herself blushing and was glad that there didn't seem to be many people about. There had been no mistaking Osian's tone. And her crying like that. So embarrassing. She could tell he thought she was behaving like a schoolgirl. When she got back to the farm, she wouldn't say anything to Mario about the colours of the spring or Italian names for daffodils, or the Commander's praise for their duet. Nor would she speak about this, this *fraternisation,* either. Because, if she did, he would know that she had done something out of the ordinary for him and she didn't want that. No, she would just let him think the letter had gone and would say no more about it. And perhaps she'd suggest to Dai that Mario was much stronger than he first appeared, so, perhaps she could spare him for work in the fields now.

But none of it made sense, really. Why did they put the POWs on farms, or encourage what they called *activities* at the camp if they didn't want you to *fraternise?* Or, put more simply, be friendly. Because that's what her feelings for Mario were, she told herself. *Friendly.* Nothing more or less.

But she wondered who had spotted the letter? Gwen, the Post Mistress? – who hadn't got a clue what was going on really. Nor would she have suspected for one moment that Mrs Dai Williams, wife of the Chair of the War Ag., was capable of performing an act of... what was it, *subterfuge, treachery?*

As she came up to the square, she saw Tommy Hamblas, the telegraph boy, going into the Post Office. It *had* been him, dressed up in the POW uniform last night. She knew it. She lifted her hand to wave, but decided against it.

Mick Scully

Until recently the subject of Mick Scully's published fiction has been crime and he was a member of The Crime Writers' Association. He is the author of *Little Moscow* (Tindal Street Press, 2007), a collection of linked stories set in the Little Moscow, a canal-side bar frequented by Birmingham's criminal fraternity, and the novel *The Norway Room* (Tindal Street Press, 2014), which chronicles an internecine war in Birmingham's underworld. He has had stories published in a number of crime fiction magazines, and was one of three writers featured in the collection *Dreams Never End* (Tindal Street Press, 2004). In 2014 his story 'The Sea in Birmingham' was included in Salt Publishing's collection *Best British Short Stories* for that year. He is currently working on a novel *Criminal Behaviour* that unlike previous work has a strong autobiographical element.

I t was in JFK in 1988 that I first met the writer. No. That's wrong – first saw the writer. Saw him. In the flesh I suppose you would say. I had just come off the flight from Heathrow. Sweaty. Tired. It was a packed aeroplane. Not enough air. Not enough plane either; no legroom. Now I could stretch my legs. Extend my arms. Breathe.

Waiting in the queue at passport control I turned my head. Looked around. A long trail of restless dishevelled tired people. The line curved, snake-like; its tail disappearing through grey double-doors, propped open.

And. At the curve of the snake – I saw him. At first I didn't recognise him. I knew I knew him – but from where? Perhaps one of the Birmingham bars I was drinking in at that time. Hall Green Race Track? I conjured scenes – but he wasn't in any of them.

Then. Memory slipped me a photograph, a photograph from a book-jacket – and I had it. I knew who he was. The man in the queue. Struggling to hold the hand of a wriggling and crying child; a girl of about four. In a red dress. Something yellow on it: dots, stars, tiny teddy bears possibly. Beside him a woman in sunglasses held the hand of an older well-behaved boy. The man said something to the woman. She was shorter than he so he bent a little. As he did so the girl pulled away. Broke free. Headed down the line wildly. He ran to catch her, lifted her into his arms. She thumped his head – bongo drums – as he returned to his place next to his wife in the queue.

I had read two of his books. The one set in Paris and the one shortlisted for the Booker. In those days I read all the books on the list each year. It was only a shortlist then. I used to enjoy taking a punt on the winner. It was always difficult to get odds from my local bookies. They had to ring head office who would call them back the next day ready for when I went in with my fiver. I never won. D.M. Thomas: *The White Hotel* 10/1. J.G. Ballard: *Empire of the Sun* 2/1. Brian Moore: *The Colour of Blood* 5/2. I never backed the Writer. In fact the year he eventually won I don't think I placed a bet at all.

The child had gone again. Between her father's long legs – and she was off. She screamed when he caught her. Carried the scream with her back to their place in the line. It was not a playful scream – playing chase and getting caught; the whoop of fun. This was a full-throated sobbing distress call. She fought her father. Fought him furiously. Tiny fists flying. He couldn't keep the writhing little body in his arms and she was down. Down – and almost away.

He must have been shouting, though no-one turned, for I see his mouth open and that of the mother too who also reaches for the child. But from that moment I recall it all soundlessly. A mute puppet show. He grabs the girl's dress.

Strikes at her legs. Slaps at her. Two three times. She dances around the strikes. Then pulls away again. Now I guess it wasn't his intention – the child in her red dress was dodging about, weaving about, dancing about – but the next blow catches her at the mouth – and she falls.

Why did no-one react? No-one speak? I saw it. I surely wasn't the only one? And this in New York where no-one stays silent. Yet I didn't hurtle down the line to protest. Didn't shout my contempt across the hall. This was the eighties, I have told myself. But still.

When sound returns. The writer has lifted the child from the ground and is holding her. The mother is fussing too. I can hear her crying. A rhythmic crying without hysteria or panic. Just hurt.

That was in February. By May I was in San Francisco staying with the artist Nazim Kemal at a house in Mission. There was an African sculptor there too – Chad from Chad. He worked out in the yard carving large bird-shapes, birds in flight – in stone.

I know it was May the nineteenth, for I still have the ticket. A Thursday. I went with Lourdes, a Mexican woman I met in the cactus market – short and happy, smiley and sexy, she made jewellery and rosary beads – to the City Lights Bookshop to hear Allen Ginsberg read. Gregory Corso, whose work I really like, was reading too. I hoped he would read *The Sacré-Coeur Café*. And he did.

They weren't allowing drink to be taken into the reading that night so Lourdes and I had a couple of beers and a smoke beforehand among the dumpsters in Alders Alley which runs alongside the bookshop. It has been cleaned up now and renamed Jack Kerouac Alley. Lourdes saw a guy she knew called Alvin – striped blazer, flat blonde hair, heavy-framed specs. Like a young David Hockney. And he joined us. He wasn't going to the reading but he said he'd gladly share a beer with us. Then I saw him for the second time. The Writer. With half a dozen other men. Crossing the alley and making for the Lights. No wife with him. No children. Just some friends.

We sat a couple of rows behind him. I thought of the red dress – it couldn't have been yellow teddy bears, probably just dots, or stars – dancing away. I thought of that small mouth, and a cry that was still soundless to me.

Then Peter Orlovsky – Ginsberg's lover – came and sat next to me. I recognised him from books I had back home. About Ginsberg. And Jack Kerouac. And others. I had read descriptions in Ginsberg's journal of him and Orlovsky fucking – and now he was sitting beside me. He nodded, Hi. I nodded back. I wondered if anyone else there had read that stuff. I wondered if the Writer had.

From the pictures I had seen of Orlovsky I knew he had been a handsome man, but he was old now. When Ginsberg came in through a side-door with Gregory Corso and everyone applauded he looked even older. His head bald, his beard grey straggly and unkempt. His eyes behind his glasses bulged. He reminded me of Marty Feldman. 'Look at those guys,' I whispered to Lourdes. 'They knew Kerouac. Neal Cassady. Burroughs. They were all mates.'

'Honey,' she said to me. 'Don't be so star struck. It's the work that counts. Only the work. And it's buddies. Buddies. You're in America now. They were buddies.'

Before the readings got underway the host who introduced herself as Camille asked us all to stand for a minute to remember and reflect upon the loss of those in the city who had died of AIDS. She gave a number – of the deaths to date – but I don't recall it now.

It was worth the extortionate fifty dollars (ten per cent going to AIDS charities) just to hear those two New York accents: a tough and droning street music I could have listened to forever. They were a double-act. Ginsberg read parts of *Howl*, most of *Kaddish*, and some of his later stuff. Corso his early works, *Bomb* and *Marriage*. I don't think he was writing much anymore by this time – he looked wrecked. And of course, *The Sacré-Coeur Café*.

But in truth it wasn't the strings and strings of words racing like traffic, buzzing like bees that got to me (impressive as they were) or the throb of rhythm (not much rhyme) but the stories the two men told of their times together/crimes together – in San Francisco of course, and in Paris. New York. Morocco and Amsterdam. Chet Baker had died that week in Amsterdam – falling from a hotel bedroom window – and both men had known him. Ginsberg had stayed in that same hotel – years ago, he said. Names tumbled like stars. Names that were stars. Jack Kerouac. William Burroughs. Gertrude Stein – and Alice B Toklas, of course. Herbert Huncke. Corso had even met Jackie Onassis.

When the poets finished and the applause died down the Writer ambled across to Ginsberg. Shook hands with him. Perhaps he was introducing himself. Perhaps they already knew each other. Were buddies. I went to the bookshelves.

I bought a copy of *Kaddish and Other Poems*. Ginsberg signed it for me. I'm looking at that signature now. Mick, I said. When he asked my name. *For Mick*, he wrote. *Enjoy my work. Allen Ginsberg. San Francisco. 05.19.88.* And when I said Thanks, Mr Ginsberg. I appreciate it: is that an Irish accent I hear?

'No. English.'

'London?'

'Birmingham.'

'You have a Birmingham there?'

'Yes.'

The Writer, now standing behind the poets talking to Orlovsky and a girl with a camera, looked over – but only for a moment – before returning to his conversation.

He had laid a sweater over the back of his seat. Grey. Cashmere. A neat yellow edge around the neck. As we were leaving I went across and got it. 'Are you stealing that?' Lourdes asked.

'He's a bastard.'

'You know him?'

'I know enough.'

Outside she was angry. 'Why would you pull a stunt like that?' Then softened a little. 'I guess it kinda suits you.'

We went for pizza in the Blue Octopus Cafeteria on Market Street. I dropped anchovies on the sweater. Spat on a napkin and tried to clean it off – but only made it worse. I was marked. Then we went to a bar for wine and finally to the twenty-four hour Virgin store so Lourdes could buy a Chet Baker CD. In the end I bought it for her. I had forgotten about him, she said.

I was still sleeping with women at the time so I asked if we could meet up again. But she said no. Not in that way. I think it was the sweater.

I would say it was a good ten years before I read anything else by the Writer. But. Before going to Russia for the first time – a holiday – I bought half a dozen novels set in Russia. One of his was one of them. *Gulag*. Very moving. Or it should have been.

You know how sometimes when you're reading you get a visual image in your head – one of the characters? So strong. Often the face of someone famous. For me, for example, Raskolnikov will always have the face of the young Tom Courtenay – as he was in *The Loneliness of the Long Distance Runner*; I had just seen the film when I read the novel for the first time. Or it can be the face of someone you know. The woman from the newsagent. And that image won't go. It becomes the face of the character. Is them. As I read of Natan, the consumptive young architect at the centre of *Gulag*, it was photographs of Allen Ginsberg as a young man that came to form the character visually for me. 'His fierce brown eyes imprisoned behind heavily framed spectacles ...' But as I read of Natan's inner roar of anguish, so compassionately told, the mime show of the child in a red dress – with its stars or teddy bears or simply dots – played out again behind the words.

Danced over them. Between them. And another image. Of the Writer himself. Photographed on the back of the book. Wearing a sweater I could swear was the one I ruined with anchovies.

When he did win the Booker – and most of the other prizes that year – I bought the book but never got round to reading it and when I quickly needed a birthday present it served that purpose very well.

I first met Ollie in a bar in Earl's Court. No. That's wrong. It was in a bar in Earl's Court that I first *saw* Ollie. I actually met him, or started talking to him, a couple of hours later on the tube. He was wearing headphones. Legs splayed for balance. Holding the straphanger. Being swayed about, swung about, by the movement of the train. He noticed me looking. Smiled. Then he smiled again. He was too young for me really – mid-twenties – but I got up and reached for the strap. Fist to fist. We sort of danced together with the rhythm of the train. I mouthed words. He lifted one speaker from his ear. Pushed his face closer. Still smiling.

'You were in the Coleherne?'

'Yeah.'

'What're you listening to?'

'A play list. All-time favourites. My top fifty. This is number thirty-four. *Egyptian Reggae*.' He pushed the speaker towards my ear so I got a snatch of the track.

'You're going back a bit. Haven't heard that in years.'

'Classic music, mate.'

It was that feeling you get. You've been waiting for this. Expecting him. Like an appointment. He told me he had a partner, at least someone he was seeing regularly. He said to come back anyway and have a beer. But ... just a beer. Of course it was more than a beer.

The next morning as Ollie made coffee I mooched his bookshelves. Not too many books. Lots of CDs. Neatly grouped. With models of Formula 1 cars working as dividers. The books were mostly about Formula 1 too. Big books of photographs. A couple on Ayrton Senna. Then. Held in place between a McLaren in red and white Marlboro livery and a silver Mercedes I saw a quartet of books by the Writer. Ollie was behind me now with the coffees. He placed mine beside me. 'D'you like his work?' I tapped the novels.

'His books you mean? Not really. He thinks I do. So he gives me them.'

'You know him?'

'I do his garden. I've got a small gardening business. The Blackheath area. Lawns, flowerbeds, small tree work. And a bit of light building. Fountains. Patios. Just me and a couple of lads I take on casual. I do Glenda Jackson's garden.'

'The actress.'

'Nah. This one's an MP. Labour.'

'She used to be an actress. Made films.'

'Did she? Cool. She's never said.'

'So what's he like? He's very successful. Sells lots of books.'

'He'd need to the rates I charge.' He chuckled. 'He's all right. I like him. You see him watching us sometimes. His study, or workroom as he calls it, backs on to the garden. I get on okay with him. He teases me that I'm going to end up in one of his books. Says that anything and everything is material for his work. He writes articles, you know. As well as novels.'

'He's got children hasn't he?'

'A son and a daughter. The son's a nice bloke. At university in America. The daughter. Naomi. You don't see much of her. She's not very well.'

I took *Gulag* from the shelf. Opened it. 'He's signed this to you.'

'Yeah. He signs them all.'

'Did he draw this? The lion?'

'I'm a Millwall supporter. He teases me about that too. He supports Chelsea.' He blinked, nervously. I hadn't noticed that before. 'Have you read his books?'

'Some. I've read this one. I thought it was good. Natan's such a great character. What he goes through. His courage. Principles. What did you think?'

'What did I think? Of the book? Nothing really.' He blinked again. There was something wrong. His fist tightened round the coffee cup. 'I haven't read it. I haven't read any of them.' Then. Brazenly. His mouth changing shape. Defiantly. 'I can't read. Not very well, anyway. Not properly. Bermondsey education for you. The river for brains. Illiterate. That's the word. Isn't it?' And he laughed hollowly. A sneer really.

What do you say? What should you say? Whatever it is I didn't. But simply turned. In the ice of the moment. And slipped *Gulag* neatly back into place. And remained. With my back to the cold silence. Then. 'These cars are good. Did you make them?'

'Yeah. From kits. Diagram instructions. Not many words. Just Fig A. Fig B. Easy to follow.'

I picked up another book: *Ayrton Senna – A Life in Pictures.* 'You liked Ayrton Senna?'

'Loved the bloke. Absolutely loved him.' When I turned he was grinning again.

He said he'd give me a lift back to where I was staying. He had to get to work. There was grass to cut, money to earn. He drove his truck like Formula 1. When he dropped me off in Acton he gave me a business card. For the number, he said. And winked. And he gave me a plant in a white pot. 'It's a kalanchoe. Put it on a window ledge. It needs light. And don't overwater it.'

When I lost my job in Birmingham I was in a mess. Ollie offered me occasional work. It was summer so he was busy. I would go down for two or three days at a time. We were just friends by now so I slept on the couch, except when Ollie was with his partner, then I was able to use his bed. That summer I must have helped him in most of his gardens, Glenda Jackson's twice. But never the writer's; it just never happened – until it did. In the autumn. Some hot days at the end of September. 'He wants some shrubs removed and a holly hedge planted,' Ollie told me over the phone. 'A couple of days work if you want it?'

An old rowan tree had to go too. Ollie was up in it sawing off branches that I dragged into a pile so that another guy, Russell, could log them. I was staring up at Ollie – shirt off and stretched out amongst the branches – privately lamenting the fact that our relationship was now purely platonic, when she emerged from the house. Naomi. The daughter. It must be. A thin girl in a black leotard. A Lowry figure carrying a yoga mat.

Slowly. With an angular clumsy elegance she made her way along the path to the lawn where she laid down the mat and started to go through her asanas. I watched her through the glare of September sunshine. One posture moving into the next. Like the animated black line from *Vision On* with Tony Hart that I used to watch after school as a kid that moved and changed seamlessly from one shape to another. From line to ball to flower to snail to whale and back to line again. I tried to recall the theme music, the gentle repetitive brush drum and guitar ... a lazily insistent beat effortlessly repeating and repeating as the line moved. As now, she, Naomi, moved. And I was moved. Recalling – as I did again – the silently running child in her red dress.

'Is that Naomi?' I asked Ollie when he jumped down from the tree. He looked to where I pointed.

'That's her. Don't see her out here much. Hey, Naomi,' he shouted. And waved. She stopped. Looked. Waved back. 'Come and say hello.' Ollie strode across the grass towards her, and I followed. 'Nice to see you out, girl,' he said. 'How you doing?'

She lifted her arm against the sunshine. She's an addict I thought. Purple eyes. Yellow along the cheekbones. Spots at the lips. Everything taut. 'I'm fine. This weather's just too good to miss.' She spoke with a smile, and a nice openness arrived in her face. 'This is Mick,' Ollie said. 'He's helping us out today. A fan of your dad's. Reads his books.'

She seemed unsure how to respond to this. Glanced at the French doors of his study. 'He's not here I'm afraid. They've gone shopping.'

When Naomi had returned to the house I crept across to the French doors. I just wanted a quick look in. To see where it happened. The work. Where Natan and his other characters were created. I couldn't see a lot – the glare of the sun darkened everything. I cupped my eyes with my hands to reduce the shadow. The room was full of books of course. Crammed with them. His desk, near the window, held pads and pens – perhaps he wrote longhand – and an ashtray. I recognised a kalanchoe in a white pot. To the side, another desk with a computer and printer. There were several pictures on the wall. Facing me, a block-print of *The Scream* by Edvard Munch. That famous painting – but without any colour.

I was to see the writer two times that afternoon. But not meet him. I have never met him. First, briefly as he carried shopping bags through the garden to the kitchen. The second when he came for a time to stand at the window. Watching. Smoking.

*

All this came up this morning. My friend, Pat Dunphy – who I told the JFK story to years ago – has sent me a cutting from last week's Irish Times. By the writer. Quite a long article. About his daughter's (whose name he doesn't use) anorexia. Apparently it killed her.

I want to end by describing her – Naomi – as she is this morning in my mind's eye. A tidy ending: she is gliding through her yoga asanas. A black shape lost in elegant soundless seamless movement. In the glare of unseasonable September sunshine. But the image won't stay. It is forced away, displaced if you like – or jostles with – other images. JFK of course: the red dress with its yellow stars – I have decided they were stars – darting and dancing before that forever silent strike. But other images rise and fall too. A young man stretched through a rowan tree. He's gone now as well. A shadowed study seen through glass where the miracle of literature happens watched over by a colourless Scream. And curiously now, San Francisco. A man carving flight in blocks of stone. Ginsberg reading. And Lourdes, the maker of rosary beads: Why would you pull a stunt like that?

Rob Ganley

Rob has been a member of Tindal Street Fiction Group since 2018. He workshopped the first draft of 'The Sea' with the Group in 2020. It was shortlisted for the prestigious international Fish Publishing Short Story Prize 2020/2021 and he has since revised it significantly.

Rob's short stories have appeared in print, online and in audio for leading independent literature titles. In recent years he's been published in print anthologies *Birmingham* (Dostoyevsky Wannabe Cities) and *Songs for the Elephant Man* (Mantle Lane Press); and in print magazines Under the Radar (Nine Arches Press) and Litro.

Rob is also a member of the Writing West Midlands Room 204 best emerging writers programme. He grew up in Coventry and lives in Rugby. He's a journalist by day, and has written and edited magazines on football, cars and campervans. He also wrote the travel guide *111 Places in Coventry That You Shouldn't Miss* (Emons Verlag, 2021) and was a contributor to *The Rough Guide to Cult Fiction* (2005).

Website: www.robganley.co.uk
X/twitter: @RobertGanley

Barbara was still striking at 70 and had the figure of a woman half her age. That's how her husband saw it.

'You've still got it, Babs.'

She smiled back at him in the mirror. While she wriggled and pulled on her dress, Tommy buttoned his shirt and clicked his heels together. He had a dashing, military bearing about him, even though he'd lost his looks more than a decade ago to an excess of sun and red wine.

On his fifth, failed attempt to tie his cravat, he swore and threw it to the ground. 'What's wrong with me, Babs? I've tied hundreds of these down the years.'

She dipped with grace, plucked it from the floor and lassoed him.

'Come here, you gorgeous man,' she said, as she looped and swooped the cravat.

It had come on earlier than they'd expected. At first he'd grown forgetful, and they'd joked about that, but more recently simple tasks threw him. He'd guess at the meaning of road signs, forget how to spell words and had developed clumsy strategies to cover his lapses. Last week they'd bumped into a neighbour they'd known for years, and Tommy had said:

'Hello! Do you know what, I'm terribly sorry, but I've forgotten your name!'

'It's George, Tommy. You know that.'

'Sorry, George, of course I know your first name. I meant your surname.'

It was a barely plausible cover-up and it was becoming more and more difficult to pass for normal.

She finished the knot and rested her hands on his chest.

'Babs, I... I'm scared...'

'I know, Tommy.'

When she kissed his shaking lips, he closed his eyes and rested his forehead on hers.

'Help me with my necklace,' said Barbara. It was the one that normally carried her engagement ring on a simple silver chain, the ring he'd given her all those years ago. The ring was on loan to Corinne. She was to marry their youngest son today. He'd been born shortly before Barbara's 40th birthday, a full ten years after their next eldest child. Born not so much in extra time as a replay, Tommy liked to joke.

'Do you remember when you proposed to me?' she said.

Tommy grinned. 'Unfortunately, I do.'

In 1959, Tommy was 18. He read the daily reports on troop activities in Singapore, Germany and Ireland to his parents over breakfast.

'I want to see the world and feel the life in me,' he said. 'I'm ready for a big adventure.'

'Good lad,' said his father.

'Just come back in one piece and settle down with a nice girl,' said his mother.

Tommy passed his medical. Rather than spend the next two weeks wishing away time while he waited for instructions to report to barracks, he went to St Ives to see his grandfather, a fisherman who lived alone in a whitewashed stone cottage in Downalong, on one of the cobbled streets that spilled out by the harbour. Tommy hung off every one of the few words he uttered. His skin was a wrinkled brown hide, and he liked to drink.

'The thing about your grandfather,' his father had warned him, 'Is that he's... well, he's remarkable.'

Tommy's grandfather was a legend in Cornish circles. He fished alone and always brought home a solid catch. Crowds gathered to watch him as he packed barrels with fish ready for transportation on the St Ives harbour. Whole crews on larger luggers fishing with nets would come home after days at sea with just a few baskets to show for it. His grandfather could be relied on for pilchards, herring, shellfish and conger eel. Other fishermen called him the Magician and tried to tease out his secrets over beers they bought him in after-hours lock-ins, but he fed them small bait. Twice he'd saved members of larger crews from boats that capsized in storms and returned them to loved ones, broken but alive.

Tommy spent the days on his grandfather's 30ft lugger named Dancer. It was hard work for small returns, but Tommy was hard-bodied with youth and loved being out in the sun and in the evenings he ran wild. He drank till late, chatted and danced with the locals into the early hours as if he understood there'd be few summers he'd have the chance to live fast.

At the start of his second week there, as he towelled himself after a swim at Porthmeor Beach, a girl caught his eye. She peered at him from behind her easel. When he stopped what he was doing and stared, she flinched and painted with furious concentration.

Tommy approached her. She had a strawberry blond Italian cut and pink-flushed cheeks. Her Breton smock – which she wore as a shirt dress over a bathing suit – brushed her thighs above the knee. He noticed she didn't once load the brush with paint from her palette as he walked the 30 paces to her.

'Hello. I'm Tommy. So, what's a girl like you doing in a nice place like this?'

He rubbed at his wet hair and smiled a big, white smile, shoulders back, chest out, perfectly at ease. The girl dropped her brush in the sand.

'Let me,' said Tommy as he stooped and handed it to her.

'I'm Barbara.' She ran a hand through her hair and squinted up at him against the setting sun.

'Pretty, very pretty,' he said, coming alongside her. 'That's quite some sunset you've captured there.'

'Thank you.'

'Where are you from?'

'I live here.'

He had assumed she was an up-country foreigner like himself.

'I've got to dash now,' he said, 'but if you're here tomorrow at this time, let me take you to a tea shop and buy you something nice.'

The next evening she was there, her hair in perfect waves and underneath her Breton smock she wore a blue gingham dress. Tommy carried her easel and they went to a tea shop where he told her about his call-up over saffron buns. She told him about her plans to become an artist like her parents and behind them the St Ives harbour sparkled.

His grandfather grunted when Tommy said he wanted to spend a few days relaxing. Tommy and Barbara walked the coast and explored coves. He showed off, diving from ever-higher shelves into the sea. She sketched him as he netted for shrimp. They giggled and whispered about the bearded beatniks who slept rough on the beach and played *Jailhouse Rock, I Walk the Line* and other songs on the guitar around campfires.

When they finally kissed, a shy silence descended.

'You smell like a green salad,' he said and she laughed. The olive oil and vinegar mix that her mother rubbed into her pale skin to stop it burning was sweeter than perfume.

Less than a week later, his father's telegram arrived.

IT'S HERE (STOP) COME HOME (STOP) YOUR FATHER

It's what he'd been waiting for, but he felt a stomach-thump.

'You're quiet,' said his grandfather at dinner that night. It was the first time Tommy recalled him starting a conversation. 'My call-up papers arrived. Tomorrow's my last day here.' Tommy pushed peas around his plate.

'That's what you want isn't it?'

Tommy didn't answer.

'What's changed? Is it that girl?

'What? No!' said Tommy.

'You can plot and plan the future all you like. Life finds a way to undo those plans.'

'What do you mean?'

'When good things come to you, see if they fit, before you send them packing.'

Tommy shook his head and moved to gather up the dishes.

'Forget the dishes. I want to show you something.'

Tommy followed him up the stone staircase to his bedroom. He sat on the bed as his grandfather rummaged in the wardrobe before emerging with a sealed bag. Inside was a black evening suit, pressed, with wing-tipped collar and silk cravat. From the breast pocket his grandfather removed a folded newspaper cutting. There was a boy in his teens who looked like Tommy, with a girl in a ball gown. They beamed and held a trophy up between them.

'That's your grandmother and me. I'm 17 in the picture. She's 18.'

'She was pretty,' said Tommy.

'I joined a dance class to be near her. We practised a whole summer for the Cornwall Ballroom Championship.' As he talked, he soft-stepped around the room, his right arm bent at the elbow, his hand cupped an imaginary partner's back, his left palm high as if to take a courtroom oath. 'And we won. But I was too shy to tell her how I felt. At the end of the summer I went away to war. When I got back, she'd married someone else.'

'What did you do, Grandad?'

'I watched her start a family. With a man two streets down. He was a fisherman too, so I saw him every day when we set sail. I saw your grandmother every evening when I got back from the harbour.'

He stopped the waltz and spoke quietly.

'She'd be hanging out washing or scrubbing the step. But every time she saw me she gave a smile and a wave. And did this pirouette.'

'So what happened?'

His face clouded.

'One day we were chasing a giant shoal out at sea. The weather turned, quicker than I'd ever seen it. I was lucky to make it back to shore. Two of the boats didn't return. They never found his body.'

Tommy coughed to clear his throat. 'What did Grandma do?'

'She tried to cope for a year or two. I watched her children get thin. Her proud house run down. The gutters slumped. Poured filthy water all down the white walls. I couldn't bear to see it.'

Tommy looked away when his grandfather's eyes softened.

'I helped her with repairs. Some food for the children. And in time we grew close. But it was years before we married.'

Tommy looked again at the picture, at the delight on their faces, then handed it back.

'So why are you bashing my ears, Grandad?'

He rubbed his beard.

'People go through life thinking they're brave. Like they can call on courage when they need it. But it's not like that. You need to be bold at every turn.'

He brushed a speck off the suit lapel and took on a look that said he'd time-travelled back through decades and felt 17 again.

'I lost years with your grandmother. I didn't tell her how I felt before I went away. The thing is, she felt the same. It was after a year. When she thought I wasn't coming back. She went to tea with the man she married.'

Tommy said nothing for a moment, then he gave his grandfather a broad smile. 'You talk too much.'

When he saw Barbara the next morning he told her it would be his last day in Cornwall.

'What happens after you finish the training?'

'I'll be posted to Ireland or Cyprus or Singapore. And I'll serve for 18 months.' It thrilled him at first to see how disappointed she was and how she dry-swallowed as her eyes filled with tears, but then it just felt cruel.

'Oh.'

'Look,' he said, taking her slender hands and holding them in his. 'Let's not be sad. Let's celebrate the wonderful two weeks we've had. We'll do something special tomorrow, something to remember this summer by.'

'An adventure?'

'Yes, an adventure. I've got to help my grandfather today, but will you meet me here on the harbour wall at six o'clock?'

They fished close to the shore in Dancer that day with a rod and line. They fished for fun. Tommy bought some fresh bread and beer and some parboiled potatoes to fry up with the catch on his grandfather's Coleman gas stove. It was mounted on gimbals with pot restraints – his grandfather had cooked for himself in every condition imaginable on the open sea.

'I fancy a nice red mullet for lunch,' said his grandfather. He baited the hook and handed the rod to Tommy, then lay on his hammock with a mug of beer in hand. He pulled his hat down over his eyes. 'Don't disappoint me, boy.'

Within twenty minutes Tommy had hooked three red mullets. They were a decent size, and their bright red skin was astonishing in the midday sun.

'What do I do with them?'

His grandfather didn't remove the hat or rise from the hammock.

'Scrape the scales off. Gut them. Clean them. Fry them in oil. Slice the potatoes and chuck them in too.'

Tommy was gutting the third fish when the knife struck something metallic. He reached inside, pulled out the entrails. There in his hand was a ring. He wiped off the blood and dried it on his shorts. He held it high and squinted as it dazzled in the light. It was a silver band, with a single gemstone, maybe a diamond, but more likely a crystal.

'Bloody hell,' he whispered. His grandfather removed the hat and took a swig of beer.

'The sea,' he said.

That evening, Barbara found him where he said he'd be, only much changed. He'd had a haircut and wore a black dinner suit and carried a bunch of flowers. He kissed her and took her hand.

'Come with me.'

He led her to the water's edge where Dancer, his grandfather's rowboat, bobbed. Inside it were half a dozen candle-lanterns and a rug spread with a picnic supper. A fisherman walking his dog on the harbour wall called down to them: 'Weather's on the turn.'

'Don't worry, I've brought you a sweater, in case you get cold,' said Tommy. Barbara giggled and let her hand trail in the water as he rowed them out to sea. Within a mile, he brought the oars in and they ate.

Barbara told him much later that all the time she was scared she'd cry and ruin everything, that she couldn't bear the thought this was their last night together and had it in mind to give herself to him. And that when Tommy grew quiet too, she felt the words begin to rise in her, but at that moment he'd leapt to his feet, then sank down on one knee.

'Barbara, will you marry me?'

Her mouth dropped open and she gasped at the ring he offered.

'It's not posh but I promise I'll get you a diamond big as the Ritz...

He went on until his knee grew numb and he had to balance himself with his hand on the stern, when Barbara finally saved him.

'Yes! Oh yes!'

The boat lurched as they scrambled to their feet. They hugged while the sun lowered and made fanciful plans about when they'd marry and where they'd live.

A sharp gust of wind sat them down again and the boat began to bob in a heel-toe fashion.

'We'd best head back,' said Tommy. He lowered the oars into their cradles and started to pull. Fifteen minutes later, he was slick with sweat. The streetlights around the harbour were lit. The water had grown choppy and Barbara's hair was wet with spray from waves that slapped the boat.

'We're not getting very far,' she said. Despite his best efforts, they'd begun to drift. He cursed in short bursts through ragged breaths.

'Don't worry Tommy, we'll send a distress signal. I... I know the boys in the coast guard. They'll get a lifeboat out to us.'

He rummaged through the equipment box under the bench at the boat's stern. There were lifejackets and a whistle, but no torch or signal flare.

'Doesn't look like Grandad gets in trouble,' he said.

'Oh Jesus, Tommy!'

When the fisherman – who'd walked his dog to the pub and was now on his way home for dinner – saw the rowboat still out at sea in the squall as the light began to fail, he raised the alarm. A tractor tugged the lifeboat across the sand to the water's edge and it was nearly dark when it pulled alongside the rowboat.

'Don't you look smart as paint!' said the crewman to Tommy, as he helped him aboard. The crewman winked at Barbara as he took her hand.

In the cabin, the coxswain looked furious and seemed about to launch into an angry tirade, when Barbara spoke.

'Dad, I'd like you to meet Tommy. He's the boy I told you and Mum about. And he's got something to ask you.'

Madrid to Manchester is three hours more or less. The late flight was the only one Corinne could afford. It meant getting in at midnight but her mum had called her dad and yelled at him all the way to the airport until he agreed not to go out with the lads and to pick Corinne up instead.

'You see, he still loves me,' she said on hanging up and burst out laughing. They'd been separated three years and even now, at 28, Corinne didn't see the funny side.

It had been a long weekend. Corinne had gone out there for a friend's wedding and took the chance to spend some time with her mum too and both nights had been late ones. She arrived at the airport early enough to get a seat with extra leg room next to an exit behind the wing so she could spread out, and she was asleep before take-off.

A loud bang woke her. The plane shuddered violently. She fumbled to switch on her reading light and saw the cabin was filling with smoke. She'd been on plenty of flights before and wasn't easily panicked, but Corinne knew something was very wrong when she saw the flight attendant's face as he hurried past her toward the cockpit. A moment later a voice came on the speakers. There was a mechanical issue, they weren't sure what was going on but prepare for an emergency landing.

Corinne's heart hammered in her chest. She couldn't take it in. She looked around at the faces of the other passengers, half-lit by the yellow downlighters. Some were frozen with dread, others had set their jaws or scrabbled beneath the seats for life jackets. She was surprised how quiet it was – no hysterics, just silence and the occasional sob. And her pulse banging in her ears.

She grabbed and read the safety card, eyed the exit door next to her, tried to recall what the attendant had told her when she'd first sat down, dog tired. She thought about her mum and dad. She felt sad she had no one else. It wasn't fair. She'd barely got started. She wasn't ready.

The pilot, this time remembering to announce himself as the captain, came on the speakers again. He said there was a problem with the engine and that they were going to aim for a nearby airport. An attendant made a dash up and down the aisle, telling people to prepare to brace when the time came. The other attendant sat and put her face in her hands. Corinne heard a wavering voice in the row behind her: 'My god, we're actually going to crash.'

Then came the captain again, urging them to brace for impact. The attendants shouted: 'Brace, brace, heads down, stay down'. Corinne scrunched herself into a ball.

The plane hit hard, then hit again and a third time, when it began to turn. Corinne had been in a car crash before, but it was nothing to this. Something hit her on the back of the head. She felt a roar of heat, then everything stopped.

It was the sirens that brought her round and she gasped for breath. It was pitch black and her head was throbbing, but she could still feel the exit door to her left. Corinne unbuckled her belt, grabbed the handle, yanked and pushed the door outward. It took all her strength to pull herself up and out, onto the wing. She patted herself down. Her cheek and eye felt crunchy but she was intact.

There was just enough light to see the plane had come to rest tangled in the perimeter fence of a small airport runway. Fire engines surrounded it and were helping people down slides from the other exit doors.

She'd survived a plane crash. What now?

Dylan and his father had been out fishing the previous evening. Dylan's father had a 30ft lugger, Dancer, left to him when his own grandfather died. It was in immaculate condition and when Dylan visited they'd set off together and spend the weekend at sea, drinking beer and gazing at the horizon. Whatever Dylan had going on in his life, there was no problem so pressing he couldn't fish his way out of it.

They'd steered clear of shipping lanes and headlands and drifted 30 or more miles out to sea. They'd gone to sleep on platforms under tents at either end of the boat. Sometimes Dylan would wake in the small hours to a sea of phosphorescence, or snorting from a pod of nearby dolphins, but this time it was a thud against the lugger's hull and it woke his father too.

'Have we run aground?' he said, disoriented.

'We're miles from land.'

The mist and cloud had begun to clear and the moon was full and cast a wobbly egg of light on their boat and the water around them, like a giant search and rescue beam. And then they saw it. A section of aeroplane wing.

'Dad, look at this, help me haul it aboard,' said Dylan, reaching for the torn slice of winglet and wrapping his hand round it. Just then a wave hit the side of the boat, jolting Dylan forward and the serrated metal where it had sheared from the plane bit deep into his palm.

The A&E was heaving.

'Why's it so busy this early?' Dylan asked the receptionist.

'A plane – forced landing at Newquay,' she said.

'Oh no – did people die?'

'Not yet,' she said.

Dylan looked at his hand, wrapped in a towel sodden with his blood.

'This doesn't seem so bad now, I'll just come back later.'

'I can't let you go looking like that. Take a seat and we'll get to you.'

There were a couple of seats in the corner, next to a woman whose face was smeared black like a chimney cleaner. They sat but after a moment's fidgeting Dylan's father spoke.

'Would you like a coffee, I'll get coffee. Can I get you a coffee?' he said to the woman. 'I'll get you a coffee,' he said before she could answer.

'I'm sorry, he hates hospitals. I'm Dylan. What are you in for?'

'I'm Corinne,' she croaked. 'Plane crash.'

She explained how she'd been flying to Manchester from Madrid and should have landed six hours ago.

'That was my father, Tommy,' he said. He noticed she was shaking. Understandably, he thought.

'It's so cold in here,' she muttered.

'Here, have this,' he said, pulling off his fisherman's sweater, sucking his teeth when the sleeve snagged on his hand wrap. She hesitated then took it and pulled it on.

He turned to look at her full in the face. Corinne smiled weakly at him, then winced from the pain of her swollen cheek. He fussed to make sure she was comfortable, nervous now he'd noticed how striking she was.

His father returned with the coffees.

'Milk and sugar?' he said.

They sipped their drinks in silence as the A&E throbbed around them.

Dylan noticed Corinne looking at his bulbous, bloodied hand. He held it up like a trophy, punched the air with it, the towel filthy and unravelling. She laughed.

'What's a boy like you doing in a nice place like this?' she said. He laughed and his father frowned.

'Dad, you might as well head home. I'll call you when I need a lift.'

It was weeks before Dylan saw her again and months before Corinne had fully recovered from the crash. It would be years still for her to stop having the nightmares.

Dylan's mother told his father he was planning to propose to Corinne, even though he'd told her not to. They knew he was struggling with his finances and in the end he proposed with the same ring his father had used for his mother back in the 1950s. But it was perfect and he hadn't needed to resize it, it fitted snugly.

'The sea,' was all Tommy could say, beaming and nodding in a knowing way, when they broke the news to them both.

'Do you think you'll ever keep your promise?' said Barbara, turning to look at Tommy.

'What promise?'

'Don't think I'll let you forget that important detail just yet...'

He hunted through memories in panic. It was like trying to capture quicksilver fish from a shoal with his bare hands, and he thought he saw in Barbara's face a sadness he'd not seen before.

'Barbara, I...' he said, and began to shake.

She rushed to him, her face filled with, what, dismay? No, it was horror and guilt. She saw that she'd spooked him. In that moment he felt the heft of their 50 years of marriage, and it came to him and he saw she'd been joking. He remembered the bold promise he'd made all those years ago.

'Barbara... I know I told you I'd replace that crappy bit of crystal with a diamond as big as the Ritz,' he said. She gasped, laughed and rained kisses all over his face. 'But a good salesman will say anything to clinch the deal.'

Gaynor Arnold

Gaynor Arnold has had three books published, as well as a number of short stories. Her debut novel *Girl in a Blue Dress* (Tindal Street Press, 2008) was longlisted for the Man Booker Prize 2008, the Orange Prize 2009 and won the historical section of the Coventry Inspiration Awards. *Girl in a Blue Dress* has been published internationally and translated into several languages and produced as an audiobook. Gaynor's collection of stories *Lying Together* (Tindal Street Press, 2011) was longlisted for the Edge Hill Prize. Her second novel, *After Such Kindness* (Tindal Street Press, 2012) is also available as an audiobook. In 2013 she co-edited Tindal Street's 30th anniversary anthology, *The Sea in Birmingham*. She has appeared at many literary festivals, been a competition judge and a speaker at book groups all over the country. More recently, she has written a Victorian courtroom novel *Chloroform* and is currently working on another set in 1920s South Wales. She lives in Edgbaston and has been a member of Tindal Street Fiction Group for 35 years.

I t was a typhoid patient again, and the town was miles away on the other side of Italy. I shook my head. I didn't want to do it. But the Signora poured me an *aperitivo* and offered me a Sobranie from the lacquered box on her desk. I took one, seduced as always by its gilded tip, the sugar-almond-coloured paper. She bent forward and lit it.

'*Grazie.*' I sat back, angling my head and puffing away the smoke. Drinking and smoking were habits I'd only taken up since living in Rome and, more particularly, since residing with the Signora, and I still felt ever so slightly fraudulent pretending it all came naturally. When I'd arrived at the clinic six months before, with my letter of recommendation and a small cardboard suitcase full of home-made summer clothes, I'd never drunk more than a sherry at Christmas. My father disapproved of young women drinking alcohol, except perhaps when *Jingle Bells* was in the air, and then only in the minutest of quantities. I often thought of him sitting in our tall, dark dining room with his solitary glass of tonic wine while I gaily downed my third glass of Chianti in my favourite café on the

Via del Corso, Mussolini's speeches crackling out from the wireless inside the bar.

The Signora clasped her hands together in her operatic way, expounding on how perfectly suitable I was for this assignment, with my English cheerfulness, my English self-discipline, my English honesty. She had no one else who could do the job so well. And the patient in question was *molto importante*.

I smiled. The clinic only ever took important patients.

I'd had no idea about this, of course, when I'd first replied to the Signora's advertisement for an English nurse. I was only a volunteer at our local hospital and spoke no Italian, so I hadn't even expected a response. But I was young and I was English, and that was what the Signora was looking for. She wanted me to come straight away. Lodgings would be provided, meals would be taken care of. The Holy Sisters would see to it all. As a result, I'd imagined the *Ospedale Santa Monica* as a kind of convent, a place of early curfews and spare, silent meals. That had somewhat dampened my spirits, but it reassured my father. 'I assume it will be safe enough,' he'd said, reading the Signora's letter carefully for the fourth or fifth time while sipping his tea. No doubt he felt there would be limited opportunity for anything approaching fun.

But it turned out that the *ospedale* was not remotely like a convent. In fact, it was the most fashionable nursing home in the city, if not the whole of Lazio. When I first saw it, its brilliant white walls half-hidden by umbrella pines, I was taken aback at its opulence. It could not have been more different from the gaunt Victorian buildings I was used to. The marble entrance steps were bordered with extravagant flower-filled urns, and somewhere I could hear a fountain splashing. Inside the glass-and-gilt doors were more flowers, more polished marble, and the pervading smell of fragrant cigarettes. The Signora – an impressive woman in a patterned silk dress – pit-patted to meet me in dainty shoes. '*Cara!*' she said, embracing me like a long-lost child. 'You look exactly as I expected!'

Her enthusiasm was disconcerting, and I was afraid that when she found out how little I knew, she would send me back to Middlesex at the double. But it only took a day or two for me to realise that, at Santa Monica, expertise was not required. None of the patients was really ill; they were there for *rilassamento* – relaxation. My main task was to wheel them into the gardens, position them under the trees, bring them drinks, books or cigarettes when required, and then wheel them back. I also arranged their bedside flowers, tidied their clothes and helped them do their hair. It was hardly difficult (the Holy Sisters did all the manual work) and I found I had plenty of free time to explore the city. I told my father, in rather hasty and scrappy letters, that I was busy viewing the Roman ruins – while in reality I was idling in pavement cafés or window-shopping at expensive boutiques, admiring the goods inside and resolving to buy myself a particular smart blue suitcase as soon as I had enough money.

I'd settled in quickly. And in four months I'd learned the language well enough to enjoy quite lengthy conversations with my patients, who were surprisingly keen to confide their entire life stories to me. And I'd learned the right disdainful phrases to put off the unwanted attentions of the waiters in the Caffè Romano.

But things had recently changed. There had been a minor typhoid outbreak in the Trastevere district, and the public infirmary had discharged some of the better-off patients to us for convalescent care. I was apprehensive. The very word 'typhoid' sounded like a plague from the past; something that would scythe us all down in days -- but the Signora was breezy, assuring us that there was absolutely no danger (*non c'è pericolo*, she emphasised) as long as we all observed the very strictest hygiene. She designated the big room overlooking the fountain as an isolation ward and put me in charge. Suddenly I was responsible for half a dozen genuinely sick people. Gone were the days of chatting and dispensing the odd codeine. Now I had to help the novices with the bedpans and soiled sheets, the endless washing and scrubbing. I was surprised at how well I managed it all. I thought maybe I was finally living up to the Signora's view of me as a competent young woman.

But now she wanted me to do it all over again.

She poured more Cinzano. 'It's the seaside, *cara*. And a yacht – you'd like to live on a yacht, wouldn't you? Especially one belonging to a millionaire?'

'Well,' I murmured, swigging back the alcohol. Imagining golden beaches, palm trees, the slap of blue sea. 'Maybe.'

The Signora smiled.

*

The town itself was utterly dreary and mediaeval, full of narrow streets with even narrower buildings. There seemed to be a bell on every narrow rooftop and each of them was clanging out of time with the others. I trudged down to the harbour, my new blue suitcase in my hand, imagining that the sea-front must surely be more attractive. But when I turned the corner, my heart sank. I had never seen anything so desolate. No promenade, no cafés, no sand. Certainly no palm trees. Just a piece of rough stony shore reinforced with huge concrete blocks and dried seaweed buzzing with iridescent flies. A few old fishing-boats with tatty sails and faded paintwork lying low and depressed in the slowly slapping water, their nets heaped in dark mounds on the deserted decks.

But the yacht was there. Pure white, looking as if it had come from another world. Its bows sharp, its chrome rails gleaming, its portholes shining with reflected afternoon sunlight, it dwarfed everything around. But I couldn't see anyone on board. Instead, sitting on a broken chair on the jetty in front of it, was a fat carabiniere. A card-table beside him. A pistol on the table. He squinted as I approached, stood up, belly protruding, pistol raised. '*Arreste, signorina!*'

I stopped. I was used to policemen with guns; they were all over the place in Rome. But this one looked a bit more officious. I dredged up my politest Italian phrases: 'I beg your pardon, Signor, but I am required to go aboard that boat. Permit me.' I pointed behind him.

He looked at me for a long time, assessing me in an insolent way: '*Inglese?*' He spoke with a strong southern accent.

'Yes.' He was clearly expecting some kind of flirting; but I just stared back.

'Are you sure, Signorina, that this is what you want to do?'

'Of course. I'm a nurse. There is a sick child. I've come specially.'

He shrugged. 'Even so, you should turn back. If you know what's good for you. That vessel is in quarantine.' He smirked again.

I hesitated. The Signora had fleetingly mentioned some 'temporary misunderstanding' with the town officials because the yacht had come from Trieste. But she was sure His Excellency would have sorted it all out by the time I got there. Except, apparently, he hadn't.

I tried to gauge the seriousness of the situation from the policeman's squinty eyes. Should I really try to board a boat that was in quarantine? Surely I was not expected to become a prisoner for the sake of this unknown child, however *importante* the father? It seemed a better idea to turn round and get the next train back to Rome, to the cafés, the Cinzano and the cool green gardens. But then again, the child needed looking after. The quarantine, surely, was just a precaution. And the yacht had a very enticing air.

I looked at the carabiniere: menacing, greasy. Then I looked at the yacht with its clean, smooth, reassuring lines. There'd be crew, cooks and maids on board. And according to the Signora, all I had to do was to assist the doctor, and see the child was clean and comfortable. I'd been looking forward to a glimpse of high society, and was not going to let this fat policeman stand in my way. '*Capisco.*' I said loftily. 'Now let me pass.' The man lowered his gun. '*Ehe, signorina.* Up to you.' He waved me on with disdain.

'*Grazie.*' I swaggered past him, and walked further down the jetty. The yacht was eerily quiet. I stood on tiptoe to see if there was anyone on deck, but there was no one. No gangplank either. I put down my suitcase, wondering how on earth I was to get on board. I shouted: '*C'è qualcuno qui?*' But my voice seemed to fade away in the dead air. The water lapped, the sun shone. No one appeared.

Suddenly there was a sharp crack behind me. A pistol. Perhaps I'd already infringed some quarantine rule simply by shouting, and was going to be arrested before I even got on board. When I turned, the policeman was pointing his weapon at the sky. He laughed. 'There you go, Signorina! That'll wake them up!' Then, seeing my horrified face, 'Oh, I hope I didn't frighten you!'

I saw then what he was up to. 'Not at all,' I said, trying to be nonchalant. But the shot had done its job. A slight figure appeared at the top rail, silhouetted against the sun. A man, darkish. A plain white shirt. 'Miss Nurse?' he called down in English.

'Yes,' I called back, in English now. My own language felt unfamiliar in my mouth. 'I've come to look after the little boy.'

'The ship is in quarantine. You understand, Miss Nurse?'

'Yes, I understand.'

The man said nothing more, just disappeared from the rail, and minutes later reappeared at eye-level. He swung back part of the barrier, pulled out a wooden plank and shoved it down towards the quay. I sensed he was not used to this kind of work. But the end of the plank dropped neatly to the ground and held firmly. He beckoned: 'Come.'

It looked perilous. Only a few yards, but rocks, boulders and grey sea menaced underneath, and the plank was rather bendy. I hesitated. I could not believe this was the way visitors got aboard.

He indicated my suitcase and I passed it to him. He then held out his other hand and led me back up the plank and onto the lower deck. I took in the immaculate paintwork, the burnished wood, the shining metal. The curious absence of anyone else.

He released my hand quickly and gave a little bow. Not like the Italians, in an exaggeratedly showy fashion -- but quietly and respectfully, almost as if he meant it. 'My name is Ibrahim,' he said. 'Welcome aboard.'

Ibrahim. That was an Arabic-sounding name. Maybe he was an Egyptian, like His Excellency. Possibly some sort of secretary. Not an ordinary seaman, to be sure.

'I'm Sandy,' I said, holding out my hand. 'Sandy Gilbert. Well, it's Alexandra really, but everybody calls me Sandy.'

He didn't smile, didn't take my hand. Just bowed again. '*Enchanté.*' Then, picking up my suitcase, 'Please come.'

I followed him down a narrow passageway, many doors either side, all shut. Ibrahim did not speak and there was not a sound anywhere. As if all the crew had disappeared. For a moment I had a vision of the famous Mary Celeste, empty cabins, half-eaten meals left on tables. A cold feeling came over me. Was everyone ill? Or was it simply siesta time, and people would appear later in fashionable clothes to sunbathe and drink cocktails?

Finally Ibrahim turned a handle, ushered me in, put down my case.

It was an elegant cabin, all black and cream paintwork with angular light fittings and deep upholstered chairs with chrome ashtrays sunk into the arms. There was a round rug in the middle of the floor with a pattern of interlocking triangles and a glittering drinks cabinet in a corner.

He indicated an adjoining door. 'The patient,' he said, putting his hands together against his cheek. 'Asleep.'

'Is the doctor with him?' I had been told there would be a doctor.

Ibrahim smiled at me, puzzled. 'I am he.'

'Oh, I beg your pardon.' I felt embarrassed. It made sense now: his serious air, his slightly reserved manner, his lack of uniform. But it was still odd that he had come to meet me, and even odder that he had carried my case. I'd always found doctors very much on their dignity in these matters. Dr Rosario at the clinic would have watched me drag three dozen suitcases across the ward before he helped me. Still, maybe things were different at sea.

'Please,' he said, bowing. 'I come back. Ten minutes.'

He left, closing the door. I unpacked my spare uniform and the satin dress I thought I might need for dinner with the captain. I washed my hands carefully with carbolic soap, combed my hair, and waited. To pass the time I looked at the framed photographs around the cabin walls. His Excellency meeting important-looking people, *Il Duce* for one. And was that Lord Mountbatten? And the famous singer in a fur collar holding onto the reins of a racehorse, men in tops hats all around her, smiling.

The doctor returned. Stood in the doorway, bowing again: 'I will show you ship.'

I laughed awkwardly, aware of the fact that he was the only person on this ship I had yet set eyes on. Surely not everyone was having a siesta? 'Do you do everything yourself, Dr Ibrahim?' I enquired, teasingly.

He nodded, solemnly. 'Yes, I do everything.'

'What about the rest of the crew? What are they up to?' I was getting an uneasy feeling.

'Gone. '

The Mary Celeste. 'What, do you mean, *gone*?'

'Flut, flut.' He waved his hands like birds flying away. They had deserted, he said. Fled the moment the boat had docked.

'What, *all* of them?'

'All, Madam.'

'The Captain too?' I had an idea that captains never left their ships.

'Alas. Captain also. He was taken by the Sindaco. We have policemen instead.' He shook his head. 'Only myself, Miss Nurse and Hassan on board now.'

'Just the three of us? *No one else at all?*' He couldn't mean it. Not in this great, huge boat. It was all too ridiculous.

He inclined his head sadly. 'Alas.'

So that was why the policeman had tried to dissuade me. What a fool I was not to have listened. Not only was I to be a virtual prisoner, but there was now no prospect of the stylish life I'd been looking forward to. I said, rather foolishly: 'But who will look after us?'

He turned: 'I show you kitchen.'

My heart sank further. Was he expecting *me* to cook? In spite of being the only daughter of a widowed father, I was far from brimming with domestic knowledge. At home, Mrs Stevenson came in at seven every day to do our breakfast, prior to making a meat pie or vegetable stew which she left on the kitchen table before she went home at three. My only role was to heat the oven and put the meal in for the required amount of time. I'd come home from school to find her notes: *Gas No 4 for 2 hrs watch it will be hot use the cloth* or *Carrots half an hr use cold water and dont forget Salt.*

'Come.' He took me down more corridors. Down more steps. He showed me the kitchen, with its metal tables and cream paintwork, and more utensils than I had ever seen. He pointed to the ovens and to the sinks as if I might not know what they were. Then he opened another door. A walk-in pantry, full of jars, tins and bottles. 'All things!' he said, with satisfaction. I glimpsed jars of tomatoes, pimentos, peas, beans, tins of every kind of meat and fish. Caviar and pâté de foie gras. There was an ice-box, too, with butter, cheese and many bottles of wine. On a shelf, bottles of vermouth, brandy and whisky. His Excellency clearly did not stint.

As Dr Ibrahim demonstrated the layout, I wondered how long since the crew had deserted, and how the doctor had let people know his plight. But the next door he opened showed a wireless transmitter, buzzing faintly. 'I send telegram,' he said, as if reading my mind. 'And His Excellency send *you*, Miss Nurse. Sorry for the inconvenience.'

Yes, I thought to myself. That was all it was: an inconvenience. His Excellency would sort it out soon, just like the Signora had said, and in no time we'd be on our way to Naples to reunite father and child.

That reminded me: 'I think I'd better meet Hassan.'

He was quite a small boy for his age. Pale from the typhoid, of course, and very thin. I could see a likeness to the glamorous woman in the photo. He summoned a wan smile for me and said in perfect English, 'Hello, are you my new nanny?'

'Not really,' I replied. 'My name is Sandy and I'm a nurse. I'll look after you while we are here and take you to your father when you are well.'

'And will you go away then?'

He looked so pathetic that I was flummoxed. 'Well, yes, I'm afraid I have to. But I expect you'll have a proper nanny very soon.'

'Yes. I always do. Sooner or later.' And he started to play listlessly with some glove puppets that were lying on his bed.

I sat with him for a while, making awkward conversation, while Dr Ibrahim stood against the wall and watched us both. Gradually Hassan began to talk a little more. He even laughed when I told him how the carabiniere had frightened me with his gunshot. 'Was it the fat one or the thin one?' he asked.

'Are there two?' I turned to the doctor. 'I only saw one.'

He nodded. 'They come. They go.'

'It was the fat one,' I said to Hassan, remembering the heavy-set face, the thick body.

'That's Marco,' said Hassan, holding up one of the puppets.

'And what's the other one called?'

He thought. 'Luca!' He waggled the other puppet.

Encouraged by his animation, I asked him if he wanted something to eat. Dr Ibrahim raised his hand and said, 'Only plain food, please Miss Nurse'.

That was fortunate. But even the thought of plain food put me in a panic. I descended to the galley, wondering what on earth I could give him. Pasta, I thought. That was starchy and would slip down. After some searching, I found a long blue packet in a cupboard. *Barilla*, it said: *750g. Miglior gusto.* It had no instructions for cooking, so I broke half the contents into pieces, added two cupfuls of water and boiled it all up. I was shocked to see how the pasta began to fatten and rise in the pan. I added more water, and then more, until the spaghetti seethed in a starchy kind of puddle at the bottom. After about a quarter of an hour, I turned it out into a colander and put a small portion in a bowl for Hassan, with a little knob of butter. I heated up a jar of green beans, too, remembering Mrs Stevenson's advice not to forget the salt. Then I sat by Hassan's bedside, helping him with his spoon and fork, wiping his mouth as he lay back with the exhaustion of eating, while Dr Ibrahim looked on, his face serious and watchful. 'He is stronger every day,' he said. 'This is the first thing he finish.'

I felt ridiculously pleased, as if I had pulled off a real feat of gastronomy, although I knew the pasta was softer and sloppier than it should have been, and tasted of almost nothing. 'Well done, Hassan,' I said, removing the bowl. 'Keep eating like this and you'll be up and about in no time.'

The child nodded. '*Up and about*,' he said. 'That's what Nanny Foster used to say.'

'She was English? Your last nanny?'

'All my nannies are English. My father says English nannies are the best.'

I guessed they'd been Norland nannies. A girl from my school had gone to train as one. Everything had to be done just so, she'd said. Even the way you folded a sheet or put on your uniform. I could suddenly see why the Signora had been so anxious to put me forward for the job. I wouldn't have put it past her to have implied to His Excellency that I was Norland-trained myself. 'I see,' I said. 'And how many nannies have you had altogether?'

Hassan considered, counting on his fingers. 'Four!' he said finally, with some triumph. 'Nanny White, Nanny Ashworth, Nanny Jones and Nanny Foster.'

My heart went out to him. 'Well, aren't you lucky,' I said lamely. 'Four of the best nannies money can buy.'

'Five. With you.'

'But I'm really a nurse.' I fingered the little watch pinned to my chest to impress upon Dr Ibrahim that I could take a pulse if required.

'I'm tired now!' sighed Hassan suddenly, falling back on the pillow. 'Will you tell me a story, Sandy? The doctor only knows Aladdin, and I'm bored with that.'

I glanced at Dr Ibrahim. He was impassive. 'I'm sure the doctor has had plenty to do without telling you stories all the time,' I said. I wondered how long he had been looking after Hassan, how they had passed the time, just the two of them. How many of Aladdin's tales had been told.

'Tell me about Robinson Crusoe!' There was an imperious tone to Hassan's voice, now. Maybe his four nannies had not always had an easy time. Maybe that was why there had been four. I was determined to be firm.

'Once you are washed and I've seen to your sheets. And then only if you are nice and quiet.' I sounded like a real nanny, I thought. Or how I imagined a nanny to be. I'd never had one myself. My father thought we'd manage better by ourselves: 'Just the two of us, eh?'

Dr Ibrahim watched me silently. I could not make out what he was thinking. Whether he approved of what I was doing and saying. As I got Hassan ready, stripping him of his sweaty, crumpled pyjamas and putting on fresh ones, I desperately tried to remember what happened in *Robinson Crusoe*. A shipwreck, yes. And making a hut. And finding Man Friday. Could I spin this out into a story? Especially with Dr Ibrahim listening? But Hassan fell asleep almost as soon as I started. Supper with the doctor was subdued in tone and stodgy in content. I'd added liberal quantities of grated cheese to the soggy mountains of leftover spaghetti, and we ate them sitting opposite each other in the galley kitchen. I had time, then, to observe him in more detail: a small, slight man, older than he had at first appeared, with streaks of silver in his tiny beard and around his temples. It was the first time I had met an Arab. I'd seen pictures of course; the photographs of Lord Carnarvon's expedition: men and boys in long robes and little round hats, toiling amid the sands of the desert. *Natives*, my father had called them as he'd turned the pages of his Royal Geographic. But the doctor was different. He wore trousers and an immaculate linen jacket. He had good lace-up shoes too, and a neat, gold watch on his left wrist. He would not have been out of place at an English cricket match, sitting on a fold-up chair, drinking tea from a china cup.

But what also occurred to me as the light inside waned and the sky outside grew dark, was that I was alone with him. And that I'd never been alone with a man before. My father had always warned me about men, how careful I needed to be, especially with foreigners; so in spite of my many outings to the shops and cafés of Rome, I had steered clear of any real encounter. I may have looked self-possessed to the Signora, but in reality, I was ignorant and inexperienced. If Dr Ibrahim were to make a pass at me, I wouldn't know what to do.

And what could I do anyway, so far from people who might help me? Up to now, he'd been meticulously polite, keeping a respectful distance between us, even when he'd helped me lift Hassan into bed. And now he was sitting with his hands close to his body, his eyes cast down as if in prayer. As he plied his spoon and fork in silence, he seemed a lot like my father.

I tried to pump him for information about life with His Excellency, hoping for some interesting anecdotes about the rich and famous; but he did not respond. Just smiled and inclined his head. But when it came to Hassan, he was more forthcoming. The child, he said, had not seen his mother for over a year. She'd been supposed to join them in Trieste, but had not come. And then Hassan had been taken ill. 'Bad water, bad food somewhere.' He shook his head. 'A mystery.'

I couldn't tell whether it was Hassan's youthful resilience or the doctor's skill that had prevented the worst. I knew that with typhoid you just had to wait and see. Dr Rosario's motto had been 'Hygiene first – and then Hope and Pray'. Hassan was getting better, but he would need care for weeks to come. I wondered how that was to be managed once we arrived in Naples. No doubt, another nanny. It just remained to be seen when the quarantine was lifted. I fervently hoped it wouldn't be too long. I wasn't sure I could endure Dr Ibrahim's silences, and the worrying uncertainty of what he was really thinking.

I locked my cabin door that night, feeling guilty, but doing it all the same because, as Mrs Stevenson frequently said, *You never know*. There was no lock between me and Hassan, so I put a little fancy chair against the door. If it fell over, I would surely hear. In the event, no one tried the lock and the chair did not fall over. When I saw the doctor's kind, serious face in the morning, I felt ashamed.

The two carabinieri continued to watch us from below, changing shifts every four hours and hallooing at the tops of their voices every morning to see if we were still alive. I got used to them: Marco, Luca, and a third who came and talked to them in a desultory way but did not stay. All three would stare at me if I appeared on deck, laughing knowingly: '*Ehe, Signorina!* How are you and the doctor getting along?'

I always waved back cheerily, *Bene, bene!* Because the doctor and I were getting on very well, establishing a routine, taking turns to care for our patient. Dr Ibrahim would give Hassan his quinine and fluid injections and take his temperature and pulse at regular intervals; and I would wash him and ease him into fresh pyjamas several times a day. In the mornings, I would scrub everything down and wash the bed-sheets with plenty of soda, and then hang them out to dry on the top deck. And in the afternoons. I would prop Hassan up on his pillows and he would tell me about his life in Paris and Monte Carlo, and his four English nannies. I'd tell him stories, too. They all came back to me; the ones my father used to tell me as he sat stiffly by my bedside in the early days after my mother had died. For the first time in my life, I wondered about him; if he'd been lonely. I wondered if he was lonely now. In his weekly letters to the *ospedale* he'd only ever spoken of whist drives and the occasional game of golf. I wondered if he'd had to heat his own meals up on Gas No 4 every night. If he'd missed the sound of my voice as I chatted away over the beef pie.

The days passed – I don't know how many – and I was dead tired every night. Once Hassan was settled and Dr Ibrahim and I had had our tasteless supper, I'd go back to my cabin, pour myself a Cinzano, sit in my luxury leather armchair and smoke like a chimney, trying to imagine myself back on the Via del Corso or in the Signora's sitting room. But one night, when I was into my third glass, with my legs sprawled over the arm of the chair, there was a sharp tap at my door. Ibrahim. Not waiting to be asked in. Staring at my legs. Oh, I thought, with a moment of panic. He is like all men after all. He will ravish me.

'You must come, Miss Nurse.' He looked severe. He indicated Hassan's room: 'Did you not hear him call?'

'No,' I mumbled, staggering to my feet, trying to put down the glass and put out the cigarette at the same time. 'I'm sorry. I was just...' How could I not have heard? I felt ashamed to see Dr Ibrahim look at me with such sorrowful eyes.

'He is crying. He desires his mother.'

I stumbled to the door. I wasn't sure what I could do. After all, I was not his mother any more than Dr Ibrahim.

'Drink some water first, please,' said Ibrahim sternly.

I nodded, and filled a glass. I could hear Hassan calling out now.

'It's Sandy' I said, opening the door. 'I'm here, sweetheart.' I didn't know where that 'sweetheart' had come from. Nor the gush of powerful feelings that enveloped me as I put my arms around him, feeling that little gulping, fluttering body. 'It's all right.'

To my amazement, he calmed down. The sobs subsided, just an occasional hiccup breaking through. I went on holding him for a long time, afraid to let him go. Then out of the dark, Dr Ibrahim spoke. 'He is asleep. You can release him now.'

I felt reluctant. His warm, moist body seemed almost part of me. 'Suppose he wakes up again and I don't hear?'

'You must listen.'

'Yes, of course.' That was what I should have been doing, not sprawling semi-drunkenly in the half-light from the angled lamp, pretending to be grown up.

A few days later I woke up to the sound of gunshots and hysterical shouting. I looked through the porthole. Marco and Luca were jumping up and down, waving papers: quarantine was over. The Sindaco was satisfied. We could go.

We were not allowed into the town. We had to have a car directly from the ship, and be spirited away to Naples non-stop. The authorities didn't mind what we did once we had left. I had thought His Excellency might have come in person to meet the son who had so recently been at death's door, but on the day we left there was only a chauffeur. Marco and Luca put back the gangway they had confiscated, and Ibrahim and I helped Hassan stumble down it to the waiting Bugatti. Hassan's large trunk and Ibrahim's small holdall were stowed in the boot along with my blue leather case. It sat there like a reminder of a life that didn't belong to me anymore.

Hassan and I sat in the back, tucked up in rugs. 'Are you excited?' I asked. 'To be seeing your father again?'

Hassan nodded. 'I suppose so. He is not much fun, but he *is* my father.'

'Yes,' I said brightly. 'And I'm sure he loves you a lot.'

He stared into his lap. 'How do you know if someone loves you?'

'You don't, always,' I said. 'Sometimes you have to wait a while to find out. Sometimes it's a surprise.'

Rachel Sambrooks

Rachel Sambrooks is a writer and performer who has been alternatively a stand up comedian, performance poet, storyteller and podcast host. She has been longlisted for the Bridport Poetry Prize, BBC Writersroom and the Writers' and Artists' Short Story prize. She's also been a finalist in So You Think You Write Funny and had writing broadcast on BBC Radio.

This story was brought to the group, workshopped and subsequently edited from the feedback. Set in the Moseley area of Birmingham in two different eras, it borders the time and location of the Tindal Street Fiction Group itself.

When they parked up on the wide boulevard by Sandhurst Road the familiar pavements jolted her for a moment. A large mature tree missing half of its trunk from the tornado of 2005, the ends of roll-ups and battered metal canisters. A roving tramp of a man with a spring in his heels passed next to the car with trousers needing a belt, looking like his clothes hadn't been washed since the nineties. He wasn't dwarfed by the huge Victorian mansions, but part of their eco-system. They were chopped up into bedsits for his residence.

In front of them an unusual, intact, six bed goliath of a house retained the original slab front steps. They were the length of a small car, worn down in the middle from the hundreds of entrances and exits. Waiting for them at the top was the estate agent, a woman in her fifties, pasty skin coated with make-up and fake tan that gave her a tinge of grey. She stood, a clipboard clenched next to her large chest. She had big hair and thick eyeliner that curled into her inner eyelids, giving her a pinched stare of intimidation but Petra refused to cave.

'Looks great, doesn't it?' Andy patted Petra on the shoulder three times. She knew the gesture meant 'This is it; I want it,' the same as on Valentine's after a routine meal with scented candles and a gift that was supposed to close the deal. They got out of the car and she shivered in the cool autumn breeze, a premonition of the change of seasons. The estate agent greeted them with no warmth and opened the front door with two keys and a twist on the lock.

In the corridor they hovered, standing on elaborate patterns of green and red tiles that stretched through the hall. A hopscotch game. The tiles upped the value of the house by a few grand, the implication.

'This property has a lovely feel about it.'

The agent's accent hid under an affectation of a higher social class but Petra picked out the vowels and pitch. The song she had lost herself. A high-pitched tone that sang up and down the words as if they were gospel. 'A lovely feel' invoked a god-like presence in the hallway. Petra suspected the lovely feel was down to central heating and scented candles – an attempt to seal the deal in the first five seconds. A lovely feel. She imagined old days of touching. She remembered this place.

The steps had given it away. The hallway more so. This house didn't give her the hint of familiarity, it was familiar. She had been here before. Her shoes were now kitten heels, business like, but back then they had been thigh high boots. She loved those boots.

Petra had struggled down this road, drunk on cider and blackcurrant, arm in arm with Emma with the pink hair. Petra's own hair was a short bob, dyed jet black and her feet squashed into heeled boots, laced up the front like an

Edwardian dominatrix. They were laughing about who they fancied of course, but the reality was both had ex-boyfriends likely to be at the party and they were both only going in case they could get a glimpse.

At the time there weren't many nightclubs the Moseley crowd could or would go to. There was little choice and the raging Ibiza-like party atmosphere of Broad Street hadn't happened yet. The council held fast with entertainment licences, keeping the city centre dead after 11pm. And Moseley had no licences either. So the pubs were filled to the brim with young people seeking adventure after midnight. If she was lucky, Petra could be invited to a lock-in, in Balsall Heath. Or you'd get invited to a Blues party that ripped the walls off with bass. But for all her street thinking, she was a middle-class girl in a world of chancers. Her father was a teacher, her mother worked for the council in a care home, they boycotted South African goods and protested for Palestine. Brought up in the enclave, a triangle of roads that meant they were a chosen few, it still backed on to a red-light district and roads that flowed with piss and beer.

Sandhurst Road was then a site for more than bedsits and mansions. The rumour went round the pubs that there was a party on Sandhurst Road. Student Marxist tenants were moving out of their end of tenancy and they hated the landlord (who didn't? – property was theft after all) and the house was 'empty'.

Petra counted thirty people she knew and another twenty pub goers wandering down the hill to the big stone slabs outside the house. Her boots brisk and clattering next to Emma's swaying gait, fuelled with a bottle of Thunderbird they swigged between them.

'And then he said he was leaving. I mean, who does that on a train? He knew he couldn't leave. I think he was only saying it to get me back because he knew I was thinking of dumping HIM.' Emma shouted but no one flinched apart from Petra. The gaggle didn't give a shit. Have to be more nonchalant than care. Have to look like it's an inconvenience to have emotions. If you see someone further down the social pecking order, you lifted your head and glanced your eye line over the top to the left and right as if searching for someone. Never dip the eyes to the person you know who's staring right at you. Never acknowledge. Deny everything.

The three-storey Victorian mansion had six of them living there. Huge garden and reception rooms like a stately home but in the midst of ratty neglected streets and the view of the city centre. That ideal way to enter any of these places, party, pub or street, was to do the perfect gaze directly over everyone's head, as if you were looking for someone much more important. Petra had felt enough of these snubs to know that if you didn't do it to someone else, it would be done to you. Even though she'd seen Nick out of the corner of her eye, sat in a corner smoking a spliff with Dave his hash dealer mate, she gazed over the top of his beautiful head, pretending she hadn't seen him. She looked around for Emma, but she had ditched her as soon as she got in and was stood talking to her ex.

The house was heaving and a can pushed into her hand from a guy in the corner who had long hair that drifted over the front of his face – another old rock reject from the 70s. She smiled sweet as only a blonde, 18-year-old could, and hovered for politeness. He didn't ask for money and so she moved on, gazing above heads until she reached the garden and could glance back at the house in relief, her eyes shaded by the night sky. It was a clear night in September, the chill had entered the air, but the noise and light from the party filled it with a heat that edged on awkward.

The garden had a few milling-about druggies and a man she recognised, one of Nick's friends. His head shaved around a small pointy Mohican, he sank a Superbrew staring into a small campfire. There was something on edge about him, even more than the bonfire he was building by throwing discarded fence panels on top of it. Nick had told her the punk was still obsessed with his ex, Lisa. How lame. Petra had seen her with a new boyfriend. Lame. She would never do that. And she swigged back from the can of Four-X, its yellow metal reflecting from the flames. The fizzy liquid gulping down her throat. She tried to push the unease away. The centre of her chest pressed under elephants of sorrow. It wasn't her fault he was always at the parties she went to.

Mohican man stared into flames in the garden as laughter floated over to them. Petra realised laughter was more likely to inflame him than to calm him. He kicked the wood until sparks flew up into the sky and for a moment the sky lit up with a glow of orange. The moment was gone. Out out brief candle.

The estate agent showed them into the front room and Petra could just make out the line of old brickwork. 'This has been thoughtfully extended,' she said, waving her arm around the room. Andy nodded with a grin, Petra noticed the signs of him grabbing this with two hands and running with it. She loved his passion but his single mindedness meant it was exhausting as well. When they'd met, he'd studied medicine but instead of becoming a doctor he took another year out and shifted into veterinary science. More money in dogs and cats, he said. He had his eye on the prize at all times. Clean shirts, pressed suits, nothing out of place.

In 1989, he would have thought of her as a slag, she was sure. By the time she got to University and was studying Politics, he'd met her as a different woman. Demure, reserved, a good listener. He never knew about Nick or her smoking marijuana or dropping trips in fields of illegal raves. He said he didn't care about her past, but she knew that meant he didn't know and didn't want to know.

When the bonfire sparked, so did the punk, raging as if they had put on some death metal. And someone obliged by playing ACDC at full volume in an ironic statement of his racing rage. He grabbed pieces of fallen fence and began flinging them onto the fire. Soon others joined in until all the slats on the floor had gone. But then he started on the actual fence, ripped it down as the laughter built up from the party. A buzz went round 'What's going on,' the energy of anarchy filling the crowd with excitement. Petra went inside to look for Emma, but in fact knew who she was looking for. She saw Emma with her ex, Tim, they were having an in-depth conversation, tears in her eyes.

'Where's Nick?' Petra shouted over the noise of the music and the screaming hordes in the garden, who by now had ripped down two thirds of the fence. Emma shrugged but Tim shouted 'He's gone. He was with Lisa.'

Shudders ran through her. She had nothing now. Anarchic rage burst into her like logs bursting in the flame. She screamed and grabbed a wooden chair, running outside with it in her hands and throwing it into the fire. Others around her stopped and watched, then cheered and joined in. Soon the furniture was in the fire, all the fence and the bonfire reached higher into the sky. Petra ran back into the house, tears welling up and a huge force like a battering ram that punched her chest. She had to find the toilet before she cried. Around her mayhem broke out, the sofa had gone and all the chairs. A kitchen table was being hauled as one of the original tenants followed shouting for them to stop.

A goth girl stood outside the downstairs loo and Petra pushed in past her, crying before she'd managed to shut the door. She swallowed great sobs that didn't stop and then threw up with passion. The spinning stopped and she sat on the floor staring at the room around her. It had Moroccan tiles and sleek white walls. The floor was a black and white chessboard. Nice. She could see herself there as an adult, enjoying this room and this riot of kids was destroying it. The goth girl patted her shoulder.

'It's got a bit crazy,' she said, in understatement that made Petra laugh.

A girl burst in, 'PIGS' she shouted and ran out. The goth girl went too, taking Petra by the hand. A gesture that moved her with the kindness of a stranger.

'One minute,' Petra said and shut the door. On the floor by the bathroom sink she'd seen something glinting. The world had gone to hell so you might as well help yourself. The lights and glimmers on her grasping hands. Sirens. An urgent escape.

'The kitchen diner has been thoughtfully renovated and extended.' The estate agent sounded as if she'd swallowed Rightmove, but Andy didn't seem to care. Petra walked through the familiar hallway down into a light and bright room, with skylights and recessed LEDs. It was made for a family and Petra smiled with the thought of it. She could imagine them here, eating a family meal at the end of the day, the twins enjoying fish fingers that she'd made from scratch. Then into the main room that was new built. The staircase rose out of the room upstairs.

'Is this new?' asked Andy

'It's from the late 1980s I believe, so not particularly old.' The estate agent was nearly spot on.

*

The bonfire lit the sky but the punk hadn't stopped and neither had the party goers. As Petra left the toilet to exit through the main living room, the staircase that had risen out of the room to upstairs was being torn down. The tenant girl was crying on the shoulder of another ashen-faced boy. Spindles and bannisters ripped with a creaking mass and the whole thing came down. Two heads popped out of the hole in the ceiling, a couple who'd sneaked upstairs for a shag now abandoned.

But the party was over. People began running before the sirens got close enough and Petra slipped out of the front, not stopped as the police had headed straight for the garden. A police car parked up had no lights on. She noticed the rock star sloping off up the hill and Piers a posh boy she knew enough to say 'Hi' to in the pub lifted a brick above his head. He chucked it at the police car windscreen with a smash.

'Hoorah,' he cried. And everyone ran.

She ran then too, following the goth girl who had waited for her, taking the back streets around the corner, with goth girl just in front. Their footsteps pounded on the pavement down the hill to where Balsall Heath met the inner city. They took a left and back up the hill. Another party had been whispered about but when they got there a police car was already positioned outside. A young woman stood in the driveway of a tidy semi-detached.

'We thought there was a party?' Petra said. The girl's arms were crossed.

'No party here. Go away.' She wasn't messing about, a police car drove up with no sirens and they hurried away.

Petra and the goth girl waved goodbye to each other and she walked alone into Moseley village to catch the night bus home.

Twenty years later and they had returned for a second viewing. Andy had one eye on the prize and Petra had an agenda. The estate agent had purple eyeliner drawn close to her eyeball on the inside rim.

'It was renovated in the 90s after an accidental house fire. Not too tragic, nobody died, but the owners decided to do it up. They still live here, it's a wonderful family home. Such a nice feel about it.' The estate agent checked her notes as if impatient for the next viewing.

'Thought it was a rental.' Petra said without thinking, sarcastic like the estate agent was spinning them a yarn.

'Not anymore.' The purple eyeliner bobbed into squinted suspicion. 'They stopped renting out I believe. They want a family to live here now. It's a desperate market, a seller's market, so you'd have to be quick.'

'It's perfect,' said Andy, putting his arm around Petra and chatting about their kids. It was all true barring the actual facts. They lived in Cheshire and wouldn't be relocating here if their lives depended on it.

The conversation was a polite lie. Petra nodded in and asked if she could use the toilet.

The black and white chessboard floor was still in place but the Moroccan tile had given way to clean white walls. The only piece of furniture to survive the fire was there too, a bathroom cabinet that Petra opened to see a small jewellery box. She was glad she remembered and slipped out the necklace that she'd looted all those years ago. A secret from another time. The sapphire glinted as if the years had never been, and all of her life was created and destroyed in that night. She wasn't the same person; she didn't love in the same way. She placed the blue into the box feeling a pang for a younger time. All property is theft after all. Petra curled her fingers around the chain and lifted it up again with a gasp, tipping it back into her pocket where it lay heavy in her palm. She couldn't put it back. They'd know it was her.

Andy smiled at her as they walked back to the car.

'I'll put in an offer.' He said and she nodded, knowing this was what they came for. 'Cash'.

His notebook had workings, numbers and discounts for potential flaws. The bedrooms would need redecorating. Kitchen updating.

'We can turn it into an HMO no problem.'

If Petra had remorse for her earlier days, she didn't feel it. It had burned away with her principles and shone in the gems in her pocket. If property was theft then they were the looters of another riot. She didn't need to feel guilty for it, everyone had to make a living. Each step down the road showed her she was right. The casualty of a man from earlier, snored as they walked by. Out of it, slumped against the wall, one hand out in surrender. Nothing to do with her. The houses on the road yawned over them as they drove away, trees crowning into an arch, asking to be taken.

Liz Kershaw

Liz Kershaw writes short and long fiction, often with a historical setting. Her Gothic novella, *The Music Maker*, was published by Mantle Lane Press in 2018. She has won three national short story competitions, has been shortlisted twice for the Historical Writers Association short story award, and has had short stories included in various anthologies. She is a member of the Writing West Midlands Room 204 scheme and recently completed a Heritage Lottery funded community project, *Our Man in the Moone*, reimagining in prose and script the first science fiction novel to be written in English. She has been a member of Tindal Street Fiction Group since 2018.

Website: www.lizkershaw.co.uk

email: liz@lizkershaw.co.uk

August 1830

For Owain, it begins each year with the bellowing of an ox. He picks his beast, assesses it for weight and wiliness, holds the nose and right horn, hooks the leg with his foot and then the ox is felled, defeated. Owain squats triumphant over its neck, his nephews shout '*da iawn Ewythr*' – 'well done, Uncle' – and the smith ties the hooves together ready for the iron *cws*. Owain's nostrils fill with the steam of fresh angry dung, the insistent tang of ox-coat.

For a few minutes, his thoughts recede. It's a relief to find his world reduced to nothing but the pricking of sweat and the pull of muscle, the subduing of an ox; to a dusty Welsh farm-yard on an August afternoon with the sun grazing his back. He wishes he could stall time as easily as he has floored his animal, but time ticks and the smith works fast: a shilling a beast, near eighty still to do. The eight crescent-shaped *cws* are soon nailed and done. Owain manoeuvres off the neck and allows the ox to stand.

He pants, acknowledging the praise, grateful that his back has not seized. It is his last ox-shoeing, a fact no one mentions.

When he joins his wife, his Gwen, by the house, she looks away and he can't see her face for the shading of her hat. He rests his hand on her arm and the bones under the striped flannel sleeve feel light and hollow as a sparrow's.

Gwen's voice is close to a whisper. 'I'm so sorry.'

'What for?'

'That I could never give you a son. That there's no one of your blood to carry on.'

Words rise, jostle, stick in Owain's throat. He nods, turns and goes back to the yard, for what use is blame or regret or longing? The word *son* threads through his mind and he imagines how it might feel if a wiry boy – dark like him, laughing grey eyes like his mother – could be here now, learning how to shoe an ox ready for the drove.

His three nephews think they will inherit in equal shares when Owain dies, but this farm by the Afon Teifi has always been worked by men of Owain's blood and the nephews are Gwen's kin. Not that he is close to dying, as far as he knows. At sixty he still covers the distance he always has around the farm, up into the hills with their far view of Cardigan Bay, but the day of his damnation could surprise him nonetheless and matters are not settled. An obsession has grown in him, rooted, twined like bindweed. It will not let him go. *Son.*

Next year, it will be the nephews droving the cattle on the three-week journey to the Welsh fair at Barnet. Owain will stay behind. He closes his eyes. Time has caught him up and out and the thought of what must happen next squeezes his gut, folds his shoulders inwards around his heart. For Owain knows a man can love two women at the same time; he has known this for thirty years. *Thou Shalt Not* ... But he has, and soon there will be a reckoning.

For Louisa, it begins each year with a whirl of cleaning. Strange woman, spring-cleaning in August, her son David teases her. She sends him off on another round of checking for leaks and rat-holes, for gaps in the fencing behind the inn; of lining up barrels in the cellar so they won't be caught short when the drovers come. She scolds him for his impertinence, but she recognises her bold spirit in his half-man, half-boy smile, and loves him for it. He is taller than her now and has soft whiskers shadowing his jaw.

The Rhydspence Inn is thickly timbered, whitewash against oak. Louisa came here at eighteen, an unbroken bride to a man twice her age, who'd widowed her at twenty. Left her to wither, three decades before, in a drunk-down inn where England meets Wales. But Louisa, solid and hardy, has thrived.

She makes sure that the mats are beaten, the sheets are boiled, the counterpanes are neat and clean. She has strong, pale arms, plump above the elbows. She relishes the feel of how they flex with the work, just as she enjoys the caress of sweat trickling between her heavy breasts and the brush of loosened hair on her neck. The days are warm, although the harvest is nearly in, and the evenings have a nip in them. Hips redden and bees laze on late honeysuckle flowers. Louisa feels excitement coiling and rejoices that she still has years of loving ahead of her. She is no different inside, despite the white weaving through her coppery hair and the thickening of her waist.

Dawn, and the oxen are stamping and blowing in the early morning mist. Four score, the best beasts bought from Owain's regular farmers and branded now with his mark. They have been all together in his field for a week or so, sorting out their hierarchy. Owain looks at his nephews arguing about who will have the spare horse, and smiles. They're not so different. Next year, the oldest – Tomos, of an age now and married – will be head drover on Owain's horse. Owain's smile twists and dies.

He hoists his leather bag. There's food for the journey and seventy of Sir Pryse Pryse's sovereigns to take to the London bank. Owain is honest, respected: the sovereigns will be safe with him provided he is not robbed. Everyone is milling around: his nephews, the local men coming along to help, their wives. Dogs yap. Children wrestle.

The half-light is cold and bleaches life from their faces. Owain turns towards the east where the sun is still sheltering behind the plateaued hills. For the next three weeks they will set off this way every morning, faces to the rising dawn; will mark each hour by the mounting and descent of the sun until they finish the day with the last rays on their backs. The first day will be short, an easy six miles from the rich soil of Owain's farm to Tregaron. Time to settle the oxen into the rhythm of following the lead beast and sorting into a line of dominance, the weakest at the end.

Is there always weakness, Owain wonders? Can a man be as weak as he is strong?

Tomos takes advantage of Owain's moment of contemplation to seize the reins of command, shouting to the man who'll check and clear the route to get going. Owain slides away from the group of men and beasts and makes his way to the stable. In the corner, his favourite sheepdog, Efa, stands and wags her tail. Her pups are sleeping nearby, a tangled heap of black and white, eight weeks old. Owain takes the biggest dog pup and tucks it into the front of his smock until only its tiny black nose shows above the stitching. Efa's brown gaze follows the pup's progress as it is held in Owain's broad calloused hand. She trusts him, makes no protest.

Owain's horse is readied now, standing at the side of the group of men. Gwen is waiting. Her small face is pinched with age and fretting about the dangers of the journey. Wisps of cobwebby hair trail from her hat. When they were first married, Owain had worried that the breeze on the hill would take her; that she would float away like thistledown and he'd lose her. His gentle Gwen. That thought had haunted him for years. Sometimes, it still does.

The pup gives a tiny muffled yip and Gwen starts.

'What's that?'

'One of Efa's pups.'

'You surely can't be thinking of taking a puppy on a drove! Why would you want to do a daft thing like that?'

Owain pretends to fuss with his horse's bridle. 'One of the innkeepers admired Efa. I said I'd give them a pup.'

'But that was a year ago. He could have a pack of dogs by now.'

'Well, if it's not wanted, I'll leave it and pick it up on the way back.'

Gwen makes a face. *Soft old man*, it says. *Too kind for your own good.* Owain knows that Gwen believes she is married to a decent man. A man who will always fulfil an obligation. He shakes his head and swats away her unspoken, undeserved praise.

Owain mounts his horse and gives the shout *'Haip!'* that they are leaving. One of the children opens the gate and they are off, a river of black and red muscle and horns. Dogs circle men wearing wide-brimmed hats and dark coats over linen smocks. Owain does not look back to see Gwen's slight figure. He knows she will watch until he is long out of sight. The pup against his chest whimpers and he whispers to it, *'quiet, little one, quiet.'* He feels its warmth against him like a promise.

The Rhydspence Inn is ready. Everything shines. Louisa sees her face in shimmering brass, bees-waxed furniture, her old silvered mirror. She looks brighter in August before the drovers come. Gleaming, as if she is lighted by candles. This year David has noticed. He sees more than he used to. Perhaps it is the rising sap in his own veins that makes him aware. Perhaps, she wonders, someone has made a sly remark. The time is coming when David will ask; she knows it will be difficult. The thought of what he might say or do if he takes it ill blunts her. She has been on borrowed joy for years.

*

At Tregaron, Owain congregates with the other drovers, catches up on news from the hills around. Who has died and who has married; the scandal of Reverend Pritchard and the farmer's wife from Fyn-y-bwlch. 'Sinful fellow,' someone says, and they all commend the Reverend to Hell.

Owain pleads weariness and heads for his bed. He sleeps with the pup's tiny body close to him on the blanket. He pours love into it like honey into a jar. Love that he can leave behind, that will stay preserved for years if it is eked out drip by precious drip.

The next day, the route takes them to Abergwesyn. The drove road slices into the hillside – fourteen miles, two mountains – crossing and recrossing the Irfon. The going is rough, and the animals need patient handling. They are four droves now after gathering at Tregaron. Four hundred beasts for eleven drovers.

There is safety in the numbers of strong, wary men with long ash staffs. Lead drovers, like Owain, have a blade concealed inside their sticks. Once, near Cirencester, his band of drovers had been ambushed on the way home by a gang of Gloucestershire men. Owain's men had put up a good fight and seen them off – apart from the leader, who'd fought on like a mad dog unchained. Owain had run him through; pushed that thin, deadly blade right into the other man's heart. They'd rolled the body into a ditch and carried on towards home. No one had spoken of it again. Owain had wanted to spill his secret to Gwen, but he'd known the picture of it would have woven into her imagination and never let her rest. The thought of him with blood drying on his hand, wiping the blade on his coat. When he'd told Louisa, she'd said nothing, had held him tight and close.

On they go after Abergwesyn, over the bare, desolate moorland of Mynydd Epynt. They take a rest at the inn at Cwm Owen, where Owain is glad of the status that earns him a bed. In the morning, Tomos complains about the ache in his shoulders from his night in the barn. Says he looks forward to next year and his bed inside. *The last time*, Owain thinks, over and over. *Whatever happens, this is the last time.* His body clenches like he has eaten something bad.

The early mist has not quite burned away when they come to the three pines marking the drove route above Erwyd and the crossing over the Wye. The other men work to marshal the beasts, driving them to swim across the low waters, wave after wave of bobbing dark heads and horns. Owain is distracted now and his body grows hot under his layers of wool and linen and wax paper and the lanolin soap smeared around his feet. It is not the warmth of the morning, although the sun is strong and harvest-yellow bright. It is the thought of that night, the news he will bring, the proposition he will make.

'Come on!' Tomos says impatiently, forgetting himself for a moment, and Owain snaps to attention He rides his horse onto the ferry, Tomos' words echoing in his ears. *Come on! Come on! Come on!*

David sees them first. Two drovers' front men, walking at their brisk vanguard pace down the hill behind the inn.

'Mam! They're here, mam!'

And Louisa comes running, tidying her cap in a panic, even though she knows he will not be here yet. She will see the dark mass of oxen churning dust from the track long before she will catch sight of the riders high above the throng.

England. One yard over the border and Owain becomes a foreigner with the distinct sounds and cadence of his language, his struggle to find English words when his emotions run high. He has long wondered whether this is how it happened, that time long ago. How it has always happened. Whether he becomes another person in the short hop across the border. A man of ambivalence who has lost the moral anchor of solid Welsh ground.

Two miles to Rhydspence, then one, and he has begun to shake. He fights to keep his face from smiling, to keep his feet from kicking into the ribs of his horse and accelerating past the run of oxen on the descending track – through the dust and stink and heat to the half-timbered building that he sees as another kind of home. And then he rides in, stiff as a starched Sunday collar, reined like a giddy colt.

Sometimes, Louisa recalls the day in August 1800 when Owain had ridden into her yard. Emotion had overtaken her that morning, a few weeks after her husband had died. Guilt that she had come to hate the hardened man who'd bruised her ripe young flesh; fear for the future. She'd allowed herself to cry it out before pulling herself together one muscle at a time. And then she'd walked out to meet the drovers, head high, her arms apart in welcome.

When she'd greeted the man with clear blue eyes and hair as glossy black as an ox-coat, she'd watched a shiver run through him as if something had caught at him, taken him over. When the drovers retired to their berths in the barn, he'd followed her upstairs. She'd opened her door and they'd locked together, stumbling towards the bed, grappling with buttons and lacings, suffocating the noise they made under the bedclothes.

He told her about his love for Gwen; in that at least, he had always been honest. And she had never asked, or begged, or pleaded. Even when, fifteen years later, she had greeted him with David in her arms, and he'd realised how much she must have borne for him on her own.

He will confess his news tonight in the dark concealment of her room; explain about Tomos taking on the drove. Now he is here, the thought of losing her – of how he will bereave her – lacerates him. His food congeals and he tastes acid in his mouth. Louisa is relaxed, pouring ale for the drovers, chivvying the maids, parrying the jokes and ribbing of the men. She is pleased with the puppy. It has curled itself into a corner and is asleep, small stomach bloated.

Tomos is full of his success at recapturing a break-out of spirited beasts that had balked at the Wye. 'See,' he tells the bar at large, 'Uncle need not worry. I'll be as good a head drover as he's been. Next year, when he's sitting by the fire with Auntie Gwen, all this done with and –'

He has no chance to finish as Louisa falters backwards, drops the jug she is carrying and slides back against the wall, ale spreading round her like golden blood.

They have lain together fifty-nine times over thirty years, tangled, talking until dawn. After that first time, Owain had wondered whether she would welcome him again, but she had. Each journey out, each journey back, he would find a bed made up for him for appearance's sake, and her own door unlocked. Fifty-nine times, his head against hers; each year their hair a little greyer, skin loosening into tiny folds and lines. At the beginning he worried he might find her with a new husband, but he has never heard talk of other men.

Sometimes, back in his farmhouse bed with Gwen, the guilt is so immense it crushes his chest into breathlessness. But until now, with Louisa, he has only felt joy in the embrace of her flesh, her acceptance of him exactly as he is. A man of goodness and of sin, a man who can kill another with a long thin blade and nurse an old sheepdog as it dies.

He has never seen her like this: distraught, abandoned, as if a vein has opened and let her courage out.

'I'm sorry, cariad. I was waiting to tell you –'

'I knew one day, but I thought we had years – you're not old –'

'I'm not young either.'

'When you leave tomorrow –'

'I'm not leaving tomorrow.'

She sits up, her thick hair falling across her bare skin. She's startled, eyes wide. 'Not leaving? But –'

'I'm not leaving tomorrow. I shall tell Tomos my back is paining, that I need rest. He can lead the drove on to the Welsh fair. But I must leave, cariad, in two days – or three, perhaps. When we are ready.'

We will never be ready, he thinks. He can see that she is already accepting, stiffening her backbone, drawing back her spirit from its temporary escape. She nods, settles down and rolls against him, hip to hip.

He swallows. 'David. The boy. My...' he rolls the word around his brain, his tongue, '*son*. I thought perhaps he might return with me.'

Again, she sits up, but now there is fire in her.

'No.'

'He can learn farming ways. I'll leave the farm to him – it's worth a tidy bit and later, he can take over the droving.'

'No.'

'I want to leave the farm to someone of my blood. And,' he hesitates, 'I thought with David almost a man now, if you had the dog for company instead –'

She wriggles away from him so she can look him full in the face. 'Have you lost your mind? The dog is consolation for losing David? And how do you think my son's life would be with your nephews? With your neighbours? With *Gwen*, if the shock doesn't kill her? The bastard, the cuckoo, given something he has not worked for? The *bastard*!' she says again and Owain flinches. 'It would be cruel. To everyone.'

The impossible fantasy he has concocted shatters into shards of reality. He sees what she's had to endure for his sake, for David's sake. How he has sinned, been loved, taken without giving.

'Do they call him bastard here?'

'Not anymore. He is my blood, Owain. He belongs.'

He closes his eyes. To ask to take her boy and leave a dog in return. To think how he would have shamed Gwen. He shakes his head and turns away. His punishment will be to bear the pain of this alone. *Father. I am too late to claim the word, he thinks. Too late.

Owain rises before dawn as Louisa feigns sleep. He will lead the drove after all, dragging his loss to the Barnet fair – feeling it settle around him as he pits his wits against buyers, surrenders Sir Pryse Pryse's sovereigns to the bank in The Strand, talk to the innkeepers and merchants he has grown to know along the way. He will suffer the weight of it through the bustle of London, the downlands, the Gloucestershire hills, the Herefordshire valleys. He will feel it cleave to him as he rides on, past the Rhydspence, over the border to home. And Gwen will never know, and Louisa will never tell, and somewhere far away, his son, blood of his blood, will build a life without him.

Alan Mahar

Alan Mahar was born and brought up on Merseyside. He spent his student years, was first employed as a librarian then as a teacher, in North London, before moving to the West Midlands to be an FE lecturer in Solihull. He has lived on the borders of Moseley and Sparkhill (with his wife and two daughters) since 1980. As a writer in residence at Tindal School in Balsall Heath he oversaw a local oral history project and in 1983 founded the writers group Tindal Street Fiction Group. His short stories appeared in London Magazine, Bete Noire and Critical Quarterly; book reviews for The Literary Review and Warwick Review, and articles for Observer, Bookseller and Birmingham Post. He is the author of two novels, *Flight Patterns* (Gollancz, 1999) and *After the Man Before* (Methuen, 2002), plus another, *Huyton Suite*, still to find its home. Between 1997 and 2012 he was Publishing Director of Tindal Street Press, Birmingham's independent literary imprint, with its prizewinning list of over sixty fiction titles earning three Man Booker listings, two Orange, three Commonwealth Writers, two Costa First novel winners, a Betty Trask and three Desmond Elliotts. Now he is a freelance editor, mostly for The Literary Consultancy.

One unexpected day off school, because the contractors had underestimated the time it would take to lay new corridor floors, I told my mother I wanted to show some other kids in 4A, friends interested in what I was interested in, some of the wildlife behind our house – because in my eyes we lived close to the countryside.

I told my mum it was a Nature Walk, and she thought that a funny idea. But it was ok with her as long as there weren't too many of us and we got the other parents' permission. I said only four of us. She wouldn't, she warned me, be cleaning the house specially, but she'd help with the sandwiches if anyone needed them. I explained that Annie could easily walk down our road to my council house, Avril lived in the next street in a flat with her mother, and Kelvin would be dropped off in his dad's car. *Just the four of you then, not the Famous Five.* No, I decided not to take our dog with us, he'd get in the way, and no Uncle Quentin, naturally. Still, enough of us for a picnic.

Annie McCardle lived up the road in the private houses – wrought-iron sunrise gate, paved drive for her dad's big Ford, mother with a friendly Northern Ireland twang. She wore blue sandals, light gold spectacles and pink gingham ribbons in her hair. She had a small gap in her two front teeth, and when she did her gentle chuckle her cheeks blushed pink. Her father was a manager at Littlewoods Pools. A tall heavy-shouldered man, I'd seen him twice, with bushy eyebrows and bright red cheeks, who must have been a kind man because of all the stamps he brought home from work squashed into fat envelopes from the firm's mail room. Luckily, Annie brought them to school for anyone like me to pick over, peel off the paper backing and half-guiltily add to their collection. Ghana, Nigeria, Jamaica, Malaya, British Honduras, Antigua – colourful stamps with beaches and rocks, exotic flowers, animals and birds, each one a bright glimpse of our Empire that was. Liverpool had been a great port in those days, connected by boat to the Atlantic sea routes, the Caribbean, right around Africa and across the Indian Ocean, as far as Australia and New Zealand.

One day our teacher Miss Hughes had the idea to assemble all the stamps Annie had donated, spread them out onto a low table and sort them into countries. Guided by Miss Hughes we traced on her sugar-paper frieze all the pink places on the Mercator world map and duly stuck pins where the stamps had originated. I could almost taste the light gum on the translucent hinges used to stick to the back of the stamp and secure the colourful picture face upwards on a page in the stamp album. It had to be the correct country, on the page where the writing at the top also told you the capital of the country and the population too. Some of the stamps still had bits of envelope attached to them, white, brown or airmail blue; those envelopes must also have contained the dream of winning big money from the football pools in our city.

Kelvin Doherty's dad was a scientist and worked in a laboratory, or what his son told us was called a lab. One day Kelvin brought a chemistry set into class and showed us his test tubes and pipettes, his powders and his crystals, white, clear and blue. He also showed us his Bunsen burner with smelly rubber tubing which Miss Hughes said he wasn't allowed to use because we didn't have a gas tap in our school and Kelvin would have to wait until grammar school for that. He was thin everywhere: his wrists and ankles especially, his face pale and frog-like. He wrote everything seriously in his neat, tiny handwriting in a wire-bound notebook, because his father had stressed the scientific importance of taking precise notes.

Avril McCall had long brown-all-over legs and was good at football, could dribble and shoot as well as any boy. Her shoe size was bigger than most of the class, and her stiff dark hair stuck out so much she tied it in two rough pigtails. She excelled at rounders and overarm bowling whenever we played cricket. She hiccupped when she laughed. She got angry if anyone told her off, even Miss Hughes. Never cried though. I expected she would probably walk faster than us and as the leader of the walk I might have to tell her to slow down to allow us time to take our notes.

My mother made egg and tomato sandwiches for anyone who hadn't brought their own and said we could share a big bottle of Corona cream soda. We promised her we'd be careful and not speak to any strangers. We were only going up the fields and back, I told her. As far as the five-bar gate near where the milestone is. It's only where I take the dog all the time. No distance. 'Well, keep an eye out for your brother, he's out there somewhere. Tell him from me his room needs a tidy.'

We climbed the fence at the bottom of our garden and followed the path behind the houses to what I designated the woods – only two lines of trees which ran alongside the golf course. I showed my fellow naturalists the tall elm trees that were so hard to climb, and the lines of oak and chestnut, and the big ash and the rowan and the shapeless willow. I proudly showed them the dens I made in the sweet-smelling ditch, cobbled together with makeshift roofs made of branches and turf and odd bits of rusted corrugated iron. We kept to the winding path, steering clear of the hawthorn hedge, the brambles and the great patches of nettles.

The first bird we saw was a blackbird, which Kelvin duly entered onto his list. Then a robin seemed to follow ahead of us, urging us onward. I pointed out the mistle thrush defiant on the fairway grass because it's bigger and greyer than the usual song thrush, fiercer too. A swallow, no two, three, swooped low across the golf course. Avril was impressed by their speed. I said these were birds you could easily draw – I was good at art at that age – and could mark even with crayons the blue wings and swallow tail, and the red at the throat, always allowing space on the paper for the white feathering underneath.

When we climbed through to the farmer's path and scanned the two barley fields we disturbed a hare which came scuttling out and stopped on the path in front of us; then it belted off at a pace and sneaked back inside the field. Further up the path it was getting sunnier, Avril complained about the heat, and we heard a battering noise – which I reckoned wasn't the usual wood pigeon flapping across the fields but something darker grey; in fact, it was four partridges, heavy-bottomed fliers, well worth the farmer shooting at them for his tea. When would we be having our sandwiches? Avril asked. 'At the five-bar gate,' I said. 'When we get there, and not before.'

At the old milestone, which told us in old-fashioned lettering the city was six miles away, we started opening our sandwiches. We hadn't quite reached the gate. I showed them the rabbit holes, only a few now since the days of myxomatosis. And where I saw a stoat loping along beneath the hedgerow hunting for fieldmice and shrews. My friends were more interested in unwrapping their greaseproof paper. Annie had Shippams, Avril banana and Kelvin ham. Annie's were triangle shaped, Avril rectangles and Kelvin quartered squares, like mine. Annie had orange juice, Avril lemonade, Kelvin dandelion and burdock. I offered my big bottle of cream soda round and only Kelvin drank from it, but it fizzed up his nose as he tried to swallow and had to let it drip onto the grass.

Avril's first idea was to play I-spy. We easily got *cloud* and *telegraph pole* and *crow*. Then Kelvin wanted to play capitals, and Annie and me were best because she knew all the names of countries from her stamp album, and I did from mine. Suddenly Avril picked some stones from the path and hurled them into the field below. She had a strong throwing arm from cricket when Miss Hughes allowed us to play at school. See that piece of pottery sticking up, that's the target. When she went to retrieve her best stones, she found in the furrows blue and white broken crockery in the soil. Annie picked out some of the best pieces and cleaned the dirt off them and said they were all willow-pattern china and squirrelled them away in her sandwich box. Kelvin wasn't interested, he'd found insulation wire of three different colours and a threepenny bit encrusted with clay. He said we might unearth a Roman coin if we had time. Or a Viking sword, if we were lucky.

Through the hawthorn hedge behind us we could sense the golfers jingling their leather golf bags on wheels, the noise of the clubs clacking together in the bag. We heard them laughing and coughing, but we could only see their heavy shoes and the back of their baggy trousers, not whose dads they were. Then it went quiet and an almighty whoosh meant they had executed their drive, with a wooden-headed club, from the tee. No applause, a cough maybe and then just the clank of golf clubs and the creak of leather again as they replaced their driver in the bag and wheeled away down the fairway. Sometimes they leave golf balls behind, I explained, and my brother finds them and sells them, sometimes before they're lost. 'But this is only a golf course,' said Avril, 'this isn't the country, is it?' I said that all we needed to do was look back at how far we'd come. We could see the backs of the houses where I lived and if you looked in the other direction you'd probably see another estate being built up ahead, but, I stressed to her, in between it was all countryside.

Annie thought she could hear lots of bees. We could all hear a loud unbroken buzzing of electricity in the wires connected to the big pylon just over the fence. We crept closer to it, which was Kelvin's idea, to hear it better but no one dared touch any of the wires. Barbed wire encircled the feet of the pylon and the concrete base. 'You always know you're connected to the city,' Kelvin said. 'You can't get far away.' We followed where the wires went, over one field, high over the hedges, above a wheatfield and a fallow field and off towards a long line of poplars. In the other direction the four lines of wires soon joined up with the town near the railway line. At the farmer's five-bar gate we stopped. We could either walk up the sandstone path which led through a cutting to the main road. Yellow gorse that smelled of coconut hugged the embankment sides of that lane. Or else press on down the fields towards the copse at the front of the new housing estate. There was a small round pond there, no trees around it, where someone, in fact, looked like two people were fishing together on the far side. I couldn't decide at that moment which way to go, or whether we'd seen enough and should go back home.

'Let's go and explore that pond down there,' said Kelvin. 'Might have newts.'

'I promised my mum this far and no further. '

'Are you scared of your mum?' asked Avril. I was scared of hers because she was fierce in her protection of her daughter. It was probably because her Jamaican dad wasn't with them, he was away. She wouldn't allow anyone picking on Avril.

'We did say we would only go as far as this gate,' said Annie.

'And I can see people by the water.'

'They're only fishermen,' said Kelvin. 'Anglers are always quiet as mice.'

I wasn't so sure. I couldn't quite see what the fishermen were like, not grown-ups though, more likely teenagers and, now that I looked, one of them seemed familiar.

We trooped down a path by a peafield. At the near edge of the pond we looked for newts and tadpoles, but Kelvin pointed out two electric-blue dragonflies stuck together. He said that's how they mated. And they only lived a really short time.

As we gradually circled the pond I recognized my brother by his slicked back hair at the sides, brylcreemed like Elvis, and the white tee shirt he wears with jeans. He's at the secondary modern and smokes wherever he likes except at home. His friend Keith lends him a fishing rod sometimes and they fish and smoke together.

'Look who it is.' My brother had spotted me. 'The *brainy* kids.'

'We're doing Nature today,' I explained. 'On a walk.'

'Aren't you *good*?' He laughed to his mate, Keith, who I guessed lived on the estate behind the pond. More overspill housing from the city into the country, like ours was and everybody else's. He sniggered through his nose and fiddled with his rod and reel, made some adjustment to the line and made his orange float bob up and down in the water.

I whispered to the others that he was my older brother and we didn't need to be frightened of him, he wouldn't harm us.

'Have you caught anything?' asked Kelvin.

Keith lifted his keep-net out of the water and showed two striped perch, spiky green and black, one of them very red around the gills.

'We had trouble getting the hook out of that one. Mightn't survive.'

Then from a wet towel on the bank he uncovered a plump brown shiny carp, all slimy scales in neat rows, half alive.

'We saw that one breaking the surface by the reeds. We baited up, then waited for ages.'

'You're not planning to eat that are you?'

'Why not? They do in Germany.'

'You'd have to kill it.' Avril said. 'Or wait for it to die.'

'That poor carp can't breathe,' said Annie, worried. 'It needs to be back in the water. I can see it there, gasping.'

'Is she your girlfriend? This pink one with the lisp?' He spoke as if Annie wasn't standing there next to me.

'No,' I said. 'Not really.' I liked Annie; she laughed when I made a joke and she said some funny things herself.

'Or maybe yours is the other one, the big dark lass?'

He assessed Avril, taller than the three of us, but in no hurry to step forward.

'They're in my class at school. We all do nature study, that's all.'

'Ask her will she come over and sit with me?' he said. 'Fishing's lonely.'

I wasn't sure what he meant. I didn't recognise the face he pulled: all leery and idiotic. 'You've got your friend Keith,' I said.

'I can show her my tackle.' He opened his eyes wide, made the same face and sniggered and made his friend laugh like a rushing gutter.

'What did your brother mean by that?' asked Avril.

'Take no notice,' I said, and shifted us round the other side of the pond to observe the waterboatmen skating with intermittent panic on the skin of the pond.

'Your brother's nothing like you, is he?' said Annie.

'He doesn't even know me,' Avril said, 'so why does he want me to sit with him? I'm going to tell my mum and she'll definitely get on to yours.'

'He only says things to try and shock you, especially out of the house. He wouldn't say them if my dad was here. He'd get a clip round the ear.'

'Your brother's horrible even if he is your brother,' she said. 'We have to go home now. Why does everyone say the country's safe?'

'We're only on the edge of the countryside, really,' I said, trying to be reassuring. 'Maybe you think the town's safer.'

I didn't really know what to say. I led us hurriedly back up to the gate, without looking back at my brother, though I could still hear him and Keith helpless now with laughing. Our group of four followed the line of beech trees and oaks towards home.

The path edged the farmer's barley fields and we were able to touch the stalks and feel their roughness and their featheriness, and it felt for a short time like we really were in the country. I pointed out a skylark twittering overhead, and the barley was nearly as high as us and stretching like a lake as far as the eye could see. I think we all felt safer to be seeing nature again, and nothing else, and we could forget the pond. It was reassuring to see Kelvin was still making his notes with his thin fingers.

We were soon pleased to see the back gardens of the street where my house was. There were the palings meant to protect the little sheds and greenhouses. Maybe, I had to admit, we hadn't quite felt we were in the country completely, but we were definitely in the woods, weren't we? And also in the fields. There were names on Kelvin's list to prove it.

'Anyway, my mum's expecting me back soon,' Annie said.

We'd walked further than I'd promised my mum. That extra part had made us late. I'd made sure we were much quicker on the walk back home. We only once stopped to watch the skylark lift its way into the sky higher and higher, and we could hear it twittering against the blue of the sky. 'That was worth seeing,' said Annie.

'But it's not really the country, is it' said Avril. 'It's only the fields at the back of your house. I mean we live right next to the park, but my mum won't let us play there. Says there are always strange men wherever you go.'

'I only said we'd see nature, and we did. Ask Kelvin.'

'My mum only said I could,' said Annie, 'if your mum knew exactly where we were going.'

'I didn't mean us to go beyond the five-bar gate,' I told them. 'It was Kelvin wanted us to go over to the pond.'

Kelvin looked shifty but not apologetic. He couldn't see the problem. He just said 'OK, easy one now: what's the capital of Hungary?' He'd quickly changed the subject, and it had worked. Avril got it right. And asked us if we knew Trinidad and Tobago. She said she had an aunt who lived there and sent her brightly coloured stamps.

Then Annie chuckled and said: 'Remember when Miss Hughes let us get all the stamps out on the table and we divided them up into countries? Well, I've had a better idea.'

She told us just as we reached the garden fence where my mum waited, not exactly cross, in fact almost quite interested, but even so her arms folded firm across her bosom. I didn't think I'd be telling her about my brother.

Annie's idea was she would collect all the flower pictures on the stamps, and Avril could have the animals, I could claim the birds and Kelvin could keep the reptiles and amphibians and the slimy fish for himself. We all liked the sound of that, because that way we got to choose the wildlife we each liked best, forget about the different countries with their boundaries and cities. That seemed a fairer way altogether, just for that moment at the bottom of my garden, and on that particular day, which was a very long time ago.

Anthony Ferner

Anthony Ferner is a retired professor of international business. He's been a member of Tindal Street Fiction Group since 2010, and has had three short novels published: *Winegarden* and *Life in Translation* (Holland Park Press), and *Inside the Bone Box*, published by Fairlight Books. A fourth novel, titled *Small Wars in Madrid*, is to be published by Fairlight Books in spring 2024.

'The Tanks' was first published as a shortlisted entry to the Irish Times 'This Means War' summer competition on 5th September 2014. Our thanks are due to the Irish Times for permission to republish in this anthology.

I

C offee is a sacrament, an affirmation of belonging, in this sun-drenched city. I love to watch the coffee-master behind the bar. He gathers the fresh roasted beans, chooses shifting mixtures of Arabica and Robusta, balances them with sensuous expertise. In his birr mill he grinds them coarse or fine. He knows how to let the grounds luxuriate in the water, hot but not boiling, offering up their heavy charge of aromas, and he adds sugar to order. We use terms from the Turkish (or is it Farsi?) for the degree of sweetness: *shad* or *morrour*, which is quite bitter, *azh*, *orta*, *tchok*. When I am pensive and inclined to linger on the past, *kuchara tchok*, the sweetest of coffees, lightens my mood. I love his pouring technique, the pot held high to build the creamy layer of foam. I anticipate the warm, bittersweet taste, the sensation of fine grounds on the tongue.

My favourite coffee house in the city is Café Tortoni, on Al Karabanchel, a winding street that drops steeply towards the sea. I went there often, after I returned from Europe, breaking off from work to spend a lazy hour in the cool interior. It was a place of regulars, so I soon became aware of a newcomer, a man who would sit and watch the coffee-master with the same attention as myself. We would exchange a discreet nod of mutual recognition: two coreligionists of this exalted rite.

One morning, he raised his head to sniff the fumes, and smiled and said, 'Imagine, in the old days they roasted the beans over open fires in the back yards, on the flat roofs.'

I nodded, remembering my childhood, before the troubles. The whole city was an olfactory pleasure dome then. I believe the aroma of coffee hits some region of the brain, of joy of course, but also of intense recollection; it sparks a sense of place, a sense of the city.

I'd been away, studying in Berlin and Lyons, but I was lured back by nostalgia for the light and for the gritty texture of the coffee, by a fading memory of the city's perfume of attar of roses and orange blossom water, by the reassuring presence of the sea. The city was rebuilding, there was a tense calm, people had started to go out again in the evenings.

The newcomer always carried an iPad. He was a man in his forties, I'd say, well-presented, carefully shaven, wearing a precise moustache. He'd sit in the corner, side-on to the flickering television. He'd motion to the black-aproned waiter who would bark an order through to the coffee-master behind the counter and return with a tray bearing a pot of dark coffee and a glass of water. If it was mid-morning, the man would sometimes have patisserie too, always the same honeyed concoction of wafer-thin layers of pastry with dates and almonds.

One day, when there were no tables free, I joined him, as if our meeting had been prearranged. He was sitting quietly with his coffee and his iPad, glancing up from time to time to look at the television. His eyes were deep brown and benevolent, and they had a frank, open quality; too frank, I thought later, the kind of frankness that hides a great deal. We talked about the first days of summer and the delights of our refreshing inland breeze — the *vent'tov*, God's air conditioning as we call it — that rolls down off the mountains. We speculated on when the weather would turn. The city always waited apprehensively for the late summer wind, the *vent'moixadu*, to blow in hot and moist off the sea, turning the place into a steamy hell.

We talked too about how the city was beginning to bustle again. Like all returners, I sensed the fingers of the past everywhere, but his conversation about the city and about the wider world was somehow bland and detached, light and airy. There was an excess — I don't know — of equanimity?

'Let's hope it lasts,' I said, 'this optimistic burst, this renewed energy.'

He smiled, in the way foreigners do when listening to your language and understanding it only imperfectly. He was not a foreigner, of course, he was one of us, with the guttural twang, the pithy expressions.

'This city has come through a lot, and we seem to have survived,' I said.

He glanced at the television, as if he hadn't heard my remark. There was news footage of tanks firing on tenements, some regional conflict that seemed to have been going on for years.

'It's a pretty intractable situation,' I said.

We both looked at the screen. I saw only the horror of war, shells pounding residential areas of a stricken metropolis. It reminded me of our own conflict. How could it not remind him too? Yet he seemed attentive to the screen, keen, absorbed, turning half round in his chair.

'That's a T-72A,' he said, 'Russian-built, it would be the export model with thinner armour – after all, it is mainly for domestic repression, no? The Russians have modernised their whole fleet, but there are client states that still buy the cut-price stuff.'

I looked at him with surprise at his knowledgeable, neutral tone. 'But these are killing machines,' I said. 'They're shelling their own people.'

'Indeed they are. It's as well the sound is turned down. But they're also excellent feats of engineering, one must learn to be dispassionate. Don't you think?'

I was unsure where he was leading me. This city was the last place where one would want to think dispassionately about conflict and bloodshed, and the killing of citizens by their compatriots.

II

It had been a reign of terror back then, during the *Tripotazo*. It had begun on the day that the season's first *vent'moixadu* blew in, the 18th August, a sweat-laden Sunday. Nearly eight years ago now.

The cars came, Minis usually, with blacked-out windows, some jacked up on their axles like cartoon vehicles. The bulging round headlights gave them the look of a wide-eyed sociopathic infant, the sort who in its chubby fingers grasps a hatpin. A mother and father would be walking along the street, holding their young child by the hand, often still a toddler, tottering along in front of the buggy in that determined way of those too young to speak. The windows of the Mini would roll down, with a faint whirring of the electric motor. And, with deliberation, the muzzle would slide forward and a single shot would be fired to the throat. There would be screams and shouting and the screeching of tyres and handbrake turns, and the smell of hot rubber on tarmac, and the child would be lying dead in blood. The distraught parents, clothes clammy and darkened with sweat, would be beating their hand against the child's breast. Some would then smash their head against the road. People recalled afterwards in the more tranquil phases of grief that, when the window wound down, they'd glimpsed a single white chrysanthemum in the flower-holder on the stylish dashboard, and smelt its astringent mausoleum odour.

In those times the war against adults was waged by a war against children. There were no orphans of the troubles, only grieving parents. The infection incubated quietly in the poorer districts. Only when it spread to the wealthier neighbourhoods did the authorities start to take measures. The newspapers every day bore photos of tiny corpses lined up in rows in makeshift morgues, their faces uncovered, blanched in death, in their ears the traditional gold studs presaging an adulthood that would never come.

Things got worse. The early ones were the lucky ones, their children died in a moment, and with them all their dreams. Even when whole kindergarten classes were rounded up by smiling men in regulation dark glasses and slaughtered in the playground, the end was brutal but swift and unambiguous. But afterwards came the phase of the kidnappings. Children were abducted and held for weeks before being left on doorsteps in the night like wounded ghosts with hollow eyes, unnameable sufferings inflicted on them. Parents had to experience every day the slow, repeated death of their children's future.

After one gruesome atrocity, the municipal governor sent armoured personnel carriers onto the streets, to restore confidence, so he said. The military vehicles patrolled the near-empty city, inspiring panic as much as security, their tracks ripping the tarmac of the great boulevards. A few days later, a Mini Estate, scissored up on its suspension, its windows smoked, drew to a halt outside the governor's palace. The back doors opened, and a rocket-propelled grenade was fired into the armour-plating of a personnel carrier. There was a silent pause, a waiting. And then came the explosion and the crepitating flames, burning alive the helpless crew. Within hours, a video clip of the incident was playing on a loop on 24-hour television channels across the world, and the governor had withdrawn his troops from the streets.

Even for those not directly affected, it was like living in a waking dream of horror from which there was no escape. The humdrum humanity of the city was stripped away until little was left but locked-in pain and fear. Even the coffee houses closed. Only gradually, through countless small acts of bravery and civic duty and the patient sifting of patterns from a million random pieces of intelligence did the city fight back and identify the insurgents and neutralise them. Then, for several months, an exhausted calm reigned, the city too done-in to move. At that point I went to Europe, to breathe, to recover.

The troubles were called the *Tripotazo*, which in our pungent dialect means the sting of a scorpion, and there are echoes of another word which denotes the collective sense of shame and violation felt when men touch up women on crowded buses or trams.

III

'I admire very much the beauty of tanks,' the man was saying as we sipped our coffees. 'I admire their technical complexity, their variety. You think there is a particular model, no? The T55, say, or the T62. But in fact each model has almost endless modifications, different camouflage, adjustments to armour, upgradings of weapons systems.... Do you follow?'

'Not really, I'm not sure I do,' I murmured.

'I see the beauty of tanks. The beauty that exists beyond the function. The meaning beyond the meaning, if you like.'

'But the form, the beauty as you call it, is the function, isn't it? Their meaning is war and destruction.'

He did not reply, but took a sip of coffee and dabbed his moustache with a paper napkin. He motioned to the waiter to bring us another round, and called out too for honey pastries. The man brought them and slid them across the table to us with an impudent grace.

'Even the barmen are losing their fear,' I said, trying to fill the silence, 'regaining their old "panache".'

'I hadn't really noticed. Look,' he said, pushing his iPad into my line of sight. 'Let me show you.'

He caressed the screen with his careful fingers.

'I manage their beauty by changing their scale. That helps control them, control the fear they inspire. You see?'

He opened a folder of photos. Photos of model tanks.

'How small are they?' I asked.

'They fit comfortably in the palm of your hand,' he said.

He clicked, enlarged, explained the significance of each rusting caterpillar track, of each design of camouflage, of each variety of gun turret. 'I assemble them from kits,' he said, 'customise them with small pieces of wood or metal that I shape in my workshop. Then I paint them.'

There were dozens of photos. His fingers swept the screen ushering in model after model. Soviet, cold war. Czech and Polish variants. Italian upgrades. US Pattons. British Challengers.... He stopped at one and dabbed his finger at the iPad. 'You see? I've captured the texture of the body armour, these plates here, it wasn't easy.'

I nodded, dazed by the profusion of detail.

'They call it ERA. Explosive Reactive Armour. You have high explosive sandwiched between two sheets of metal. When a missile is fired at you, the slab of explosive detonates and this disrupts the missile's attempt to penetrate you.'

'Interesting,' I responded, uneasy that he'd said fired at you, not fired at it. Penetrate you, not penetrate it.

'Yes,' he continued, 'And because the plates are moving, at every moment of attempted penetration the missile has to cut through fresh metal so it never gains entry to your interior.' He stabbed his index finger through the air as he spoke, his eyes gleaming. 'And if it does breach your defences, it's spent and exhausted. Too exhausted to cause damage to those delicate soft tissues within.'

'To the people... the personnel in the tank, you mean?'

'Yes.'

I considered the photo. 'So much ingenuity and energy expended in the pursuit of violence, and the avoidance of it.'

He shrugged.

'So,' I said, 'don't the weapons designers simply design a more penetrating missile to overcome this effect?'

'Yes, of course. They try. It's a mini-arms race. They're always attempting to overcome your defences. You are always attempting to overcome their overcoming, as it were.'

He swooshed his fingers over the screen, enlarging the high-definition images still further. It was amazing how he had managed to capture through careful painting each rivet in the body armour.

'The trick,' he said, as if reading my thoughts, 'is to make adjustments for scale. If you painted as if painting life-size, it would never work. It's an art to get it perfect. I use a good magnifier, of course, and very fine brushes.'

'How many hours do you spend on this, on one tank?'

'Many. Thirty perhaps. If it's complicated, forty or fifty, or this, let me show you — this one was very tricky, with the camouflage netting, and you see here, the rust on the tracks, this took me over a hundred hours. It's a lifetime's endeavour, you could say.' He smiled. There was something practised about his smile, not false, yet not spontaneous.

'Astonishing,' I said. 'The attention to detail is truly astonishing.'

I registered that he'd slyly abducted me into his world, engaging with something that held, so I thought, no interest for me. These scale models were strangely compelling in their miniature perfection that caught and incorporated all the dents and scratches and mud and dust, and streaks of rust, of the real world of battle-worn military hardware.

And then it happened, like a warp in that small world, catching him unawares, extinguishing his even smile, startling his placid eyes.

Amid the tanks, suddenly, this photo, so out of place, shocking in its way, this soft, gentle photograph. It was of a little girl, about three years old, with curly hair bleached blonde by the sun and the sea, her brown eyes laughing, innocent, the front teeth milky white and gappy in their pink gums; the dimple in her cheek; the gold studs in her ears.

The man looked confounded, his pained eyes staring at the screen, his mouth hanging open.

'Not a tank,' I said, stupidly.

He did not respond.

'Your daughter?' I ventured.

He made an awkward noise, a sort of strained rattle in the throat, not replying to my question, and with swift wipes of his finger dragged the image out of the folder and dropped it into another.

'My wife,' he said at last, 'she doesn't understand the technology, she doesn't understand folders. I like to put things in their places, but she is a little disorderly, untidy. I keep telling her, I'll buy you your own iPad. Order, keeping things straight, it makes life easier. But, you know, she really doesn't get it...'

He trailed away, and in that moment I understood, I saw the inward dullness of his gaze, his eternal attempt to move the point of impact, to avoid the penetrating missile. I could not look him in the eye, afraid that his defences had been breached, and that a raw flayed persona lay within. I felt chill, and all the horror of the *Tripotazo* came flooding back. Expressions flickered like static on a screen across the man's disintegrating face.

He had not said a further word when he moved back his chair to stand up. He nodded politely and took his leave, his hand clutching the iPad tight to his chest.

I sat watching the tanks on the television, and grew pensive, and called to the waiter to bring me a sweet, sweet pot of *kuchara tchok*.

Thursday Nights: Novel Extracts

Yasmin Ali

Yasmin Ali joined Tindal Street Fiction Group in January 2013. She is a blogger and writer. She has had short stories published in the following anthologies: *Written In Blood*, edited by Lindsay Ashford and Caroline Oakley (Honno 2009); *Cut on the Bias*, edited by Stephanie Tillotson (Honno 2010); and *A Midlands Odyssey*, edited by Elisabeth Charis, Polly Stoker and Jonathan Davidson (Nine Arches Press).

Another story, 'Perfect day', was commissioned by the West Midlands Readers' Network for Dudley Crime Reading Group, and made available in pamphlet form from WMRN.

She was one of the international group of writers who wrote an experimental novel, *Circ* (Pigeon Park Press, 2014). She has appeared at the Birmingham Literature Festival, and the Wolverhampton Literature Festival. Yasmin has also written for the stage, latterly for the Twelve Angry Women review at the Brighton Dome in 2016.

Website: http://yasminaliwrites.wordpress.com

The Lake Dal Coffee Bar's brash exterior, is confidently modern, unlike the Victorian pubs around it. Nonetheless, it is just as much a male space. Which is not to say that women don't go there; but it takes a certain nerve, or recklessness.

The interior is dimly lit. There are murals on the walls, idealised scenes of Lake Dal, populated by voluptuous, doe-eyed women, dupattas slipping from their heads, floating off on a jasmine-scented breeze. At the tables more tea is consumed than coffee, thick dark chai, made with cinnamon, cardamom, and evaporated milk. It is served in shallow, transparent Pyrex cups, accompanied by jalebi, still warm from the fryer. Everyone is smoking, but Farouk will not permit paan to be used on the premises. He says betel nut is just for old men, but everyone knows the real reason for the ban is to preserve his precious murals from the blood red spittle stains that would surely follow the unrestricted chewing of spiced nut and leaf.

Few other restrictions apply at the Lake Dal. Men play cards for money. Goods and services are traded. Work permits, and travel documents, some genuine, change hands. Over in the alcove, under a waterfall scene, Master works as a translator and scribe, quack lawyer and counsellor. He is always in demand.

Farouk nods at Raffy as he enters the cafe. It is less a greeting than a routine signal that tea will be brought to his table shortly. Raffy looks around before selecting where to sit; there are people he is keen to avoid, but today his mission is to be seen. The American girl is meeting him here.

Conversation drops as the woman, a little hesitant, opens the door to the cafe. The boy bringing Raffy's tea stops in surprise to look. Something about her is not quite right. The men know this, though they would be hard-pressed to say why. She's young, slight, and her hair hangs loose about her shoulders, much like the others who occasionally brave the Lake Dal in search of an errant boyfriend. Perhaps it's her hair, not mousey brown or brittle peroxide, but California blonde? Or the absence of blue eye shadow and pale pink lipstick? The flat, buffalo hide sandals that only village women wear?

Susie weaves her way cautiously through smoke and men. Raffy raises a hand to indicate his presence to her. Farouk's boy begins to pour more tea for their new visitor.

'Hey, Raffy, thanks for meeting me here!' says Susie. Raffy nods scarcely perceptibly, lowering his eyes. When Bibi had first brought Susie to their room, he had given her presence little thought. These English girls, they did things like that, wandering into one another's homes, in front of men they did not know, laughing, smoking, telling jokes he could not understand. He has come to the belief, over the last few days, that

Susie is not like those other women. She is American. That, in itself, separates her from the other girls he has come to know.

Above all, Susie has a camera. He has watched, rapt, at the easy manner she has with lenses, filters, changing rolls of film. These are not skills he anticipates in a woman. Raffy is fascinated by mechanical things; back home he worked with his father, apprenticed from boyhood. It was not a place where components were made on production lines, boxed, and shipped for easy use. They had to make their own parts, from the largest, bashed out on the anvil, to the most delicate and intricate, constructed with tiny implements under magnification. It was absorbing work, and he missed it. He'd have liked to have taken Susie's camera apart, to examine the inside, but this thought he had kept to himself.

Susie accepts the cup of sweet, spiced tea, smiling at Farouk's boy. She reaches into her big suede bag and pulls out a notebook. 'So, Raffy,' she says. She smiles again, a wide, encouraging smile. Her teeth, thinks Raffy. Her teeth are so white, so straight. She speaks again. 'Will you tell me about yourself? Where do you come from? What do you do?'

Raffy is appalled. These are not questions anyone asks here. Not unless they are from the same clan, or from the authorities. 'I am not interesting,' says Raffy.

'I'm interested,' says Susie. 'Are you from Pakistan?'

'No,' says Raffy.

'No?' says Susie. 'So where do you come from?'

'Africa.'

'Oh,' says Susie. 'East Africa? Kenya?'

'Mombasa,' says Raffy. He pauses. 'I will not talk about this.'

'No, of course not. I understand.'

'I am now from England.'

'But before you came here? What did you do in Mombasa?'

'I live.'

'Did you have a job? Were you a student?'

'Engineer.'

'You were studying engineering? That's great,' says Susie brightly. 'And will you go back to school here? To get engineering qualifications?'

'I can't work here,' says Raffy, his breathing becoming shallow. He lays his hands on the table, glances from side to side, as though he is about to push himself up from the table, to walk away.

'Hey, it's OK,' says Susie, leaning forward in concern. Raffy leans back in his chair. He is conscious again of where they are. He can't afford to look weak, fearful, least of all in the company of a woman.

Susie is unaware of the reasons for the man's anxiety. She wants to smooth things out between them, to calm Raffy, to get on with her work. 'We can talk another time, maybe? So. Is it alright for me to take pictures in here? Who do I need to ask?'

Raffy has no idea what she is saying. She is an American with a camera. Whose permission does she need to do anything? Susie stands. The men in the cafe appraise her, as she walks to the counter, speaks to the boy. The boy calls out to Farouk.

Farouk appears from behind a curtain of multi-coloured plastic strips. There's a swagger to the man. Unlike the dark, undemonstrative clothing worn by most of the other men in the room, Farouk looks dressed for a night at the Rum Runner. He wears a tan suit, double-breasted, and a slim, striped shirt, open necked. His abundant black hair reaches in carefully coiffed waves down to the tip of his shirt collar. He sports sideburns; not thin, apologetic ones; his is the facial hair of a man about town.

'You are the young lady who wants to speak to me?' says Farouk.

'Yes,' says Susie. 'Thank you. My name's Susan Galchen.' She holds out her hand. Farouk hesitates for a moment, amused, before shaking it in formal greeting. 'I'm a graduate student at Birmingham University', she continues. 'Cultural Studies. I'd really appreciate it if I could take some photographs in here?'

'You are educated?' says Farouk. 'Why do you want to take photographs here? Stratford is not very far away. Very cultural, very nice.'

'I've been to Stratford-upon-Avon. As a tourist. But for my scholarly work I am documenting the local community here, in Balsall Heath. That's why I'd like to take photographs in your cafe. The Lake Dal Coffee Bar is a famous local institution.'

'Famous, yes! We are famous,' Farouk is laughing now. 'We will be famous because of you. You will take our pictures to America.'

'So I can take photographs in here? Right?'

'Take my photo. When my customers see that I am happy for the American lady to take a picture of me, they will also be happy. But,' at this Farouk lowers his voice.' You see Master? The man over there, yes, under the waterfall. You must not take a picture of him.'

Susie makes a show of photographing Farouk. She is not too certain whether she is indulging his vanity, or whether it is he who is generously signalling the acceptability of her presence and purpose on the premises. He steps out of the front door to be photographed under his cafe's illuminated sign. He clears a table by his favourite painted scene, the one with the houseboats in the sunset, and sits, commanding an elaborate brass hookah to be brought to his side. The men at the other tables watch this performance with due attention. Farouk is an important man, and the Lake Dal is far from his only business interest.

Once she has completed her work with the proprietor, Susie goes back into unseen observer mode, quickly shooting a roll of film. She captures Raffy when he is not looking; a smaller, sadder figure than he manages to strike when he is aware that the lens points in his direction. The other men, an undifferentiated mass of testosterone when she had first entered the cafe, become, through the camera, individuals. One browses a newspaper printed in an unfamiliar script; another lifts a cup to his lips. At a corner table a group of young men raise their voices in what seems to be heated argument with an older man in a hat. It is what she came to do. Packing away the camera, Susie slips away from the scene.

She sets off at a brisk pace. The arrangement was that after meeting Raffy in The Lake Dal Coffee House, Susie would call on Bibi, who was to take her to meet her family.

Bibi's not at home when Susie calls. This is no surprise. Their agreement to meet is understood on both sides to be more vague intention than commitment. In any case, Bibi has no clock, or wristwatch, and whilst her days have patterns, they have little structure. Susie decides to take a walk. Nearby there is a park. She still finds it a surprise and a delight that this neighbourhood, for all its material hardships, has several open, green spaces for people to walk, for children to play. There are mature trees, some already in leaf, others speckled in bud. Squirrels dart along any plane, vertical or horizontal. There's an ornamental lake hosting mallards, and coots, and Canada geese. The sound of the main road is muted here, a low rumble under the birdsong.

Susie sits on a bench by the lake. There is a hint of summer in the air; a certain warmth that is not dependent on the sun breaking clear of the clouds. This is not her home, with its heat, its expansive, optimistic light; but after a Midlands winter, and a wet spring, she feels as though the future might be on their side. On the side of Bibi, and Raffy, and their child. On the side of the women and their infant children in the playground to her right. On the side of the group of young black men playing cricket in the distance. On the side of this place, being re-made around them. Susie sits, looks, at these new people from all around the world, new homes rising up into the sky, a new cityscape, bright and bold. What is she doing here?

It's not a moment of self-doubt. When Susie had boarded her Pan Am flight last year for her first trip to Europe, alone and bound for a university on the other side of the Atlantic Ocean, she had wondered quite what she was doing. Her mother thought she was crazy. Susie had graduated from university in California, which, in her mother's eyes had been more than enough education for any girl. Her fiancé had not been encouraging. But it was all working out far better than she could have hoped. Her department at the university is a radical place, exactly as she had hoped. It's headed by a professor who is famous for defending freedom of expression, and her supervisor is already an emerging star in his new field. Susie is thinking instead about those things which will not end up being discussed in her thesis. Friendships, rapport, fear, revulsion; she has in her time in this city seen, or felt, things which challenge the breadth of her sympathies. Perhaps if she had been on the Freedom Marches? She'd heard older activists talk of those times, of their first, disturbing experiences of vulnerability, of fleeting friendships that might have been, but never would be.

She looks up from her moment of introspection, and there she is: Bibi, walking along the path towards the lake. Susie grabs her bag, and springs up, calling Bibi's name. Bibi stops, lifts one hand from the pram she is pushing, and half-waves, half-shields her eyes from the early afternoon sun.

Natalie White

In 2011 Natalie won second prize in the Writers' Forum magazine for her short story 'Polar Opposites' and in 2013 her story 'Beneath the Surface' was published in Tindal Street Fiction Group's *The Sea in Birmingham*. 'Clear as glass', one of the winning stories of the Mantle Arts writing competition, was published in *Songs for the Elephant Man* in 2019, and 'The Wall around you' was published in the Dostoyevsy Wannabe Cities *Birmingham* collection. 'Left Hanging' is in Momaya Press' short story review, *The Outsiders*. The online journal, Literary Veganism, recently published her short story, 'A Cat May Look At A King' and the website Storyshares, 'The Volunteers'. Her novel *The Forgotten People* was longlisted for the Bridport prize and reached the top 20 out of 1,196 entries in 2018. It is soon to be published by Matar publishing house. These chapters are work in progress, and the finished novel may present this section differently.

Natalie writes blogs regularly for The Times of Israel, https://blogs.timesofisrael.com/author/shoshana-lavan. Her website is https://shoshana03.wixsite.com/website.

1.

London, 1936

The meeting in Kentish Town had just finished. Now Mosley was heading to Trafalgar square; the lads were marching down Tottenham Court Road to join him. With them, hundreds of foot and mounted police. The hostile crowd of anti-fascists was gradually increasing, not that this bothered Harold. The beers in the sunshine with his friends waiting for the meeting to begin had had a lasting effect. And as usual, Freddy had his knuckledusters to hand.

Mosley's chauffeur drove his car very slowly.

'Trafalgar Square is the site of our very first meeting! Here's to British decency and British values! Our victory is certain!' Mosley declared over a megaphone.

He smiled at the crowds and they cheered. But all of a sudden, a gang of students threw something at him. Harold sucked in his breath. Thank goodness whatever it was hit the amplifier and bounced off.

'Oh my God!' Mosley's swearing could be heard over the constant disruptions from the crowds.

'They could have killed him, the bastards!' Freddy exclaimed. His freckles had been accentuated by the sun and his face was red, a few shades darker than his hair.

'Well, we ain't just gonna stand and watch, are we?' Phil was grinning dangerously. He had a small build, but fierce energy.

It all happened so quickly. One minute they were on the Tottenham Court Road, the next they were swept away to St Martin's church in the rush of spectators, where people were throwing confetti over a waiting crowd. Or so it seemed. But the tiny, gummed labels were pieces of communist propaganda. Harold and the boys furiously wiped the labels off their shirt collars and took off their caps to be rid of them. They raised their angry fists in the air with thousands of others, amongst the whistling and hissing.

As the crowds packed together, Harold and his friends swerved in and out, desperately trying to follow the gang who had attacked Mosley's car. Harold glimpsed a sudden flash of red; the boys with their ridiculous skullcaps were running down one of the side streets. He broke away from the crowd, pulling Freddy with him, and gestured for the others to join, chanting, 'The Yids, the Yids, we must get rid of the Yids!'

The next fifteen minutes were so breathless, Harold had trouble recalling them, like moments of a dream. The youths ran into a barricaded side street, and were finally cornered. Harold's group was bigger. But still they invited a fight, screeching 'Down with Fascism!' and brandishing their fists. One of them added, 'Go and join the German army!'

Harold remembered a sudden lull, but then one of them caught sight of Freddy's knuckledusters and tried to run. Harold, suddenly aware of his chance, tripped him up and started to hit him, the boy beneath him floundering. 'This is for Mosley!' he kept thinking. 'The commie bastards could have killed him!' He punched and kicked the boy at his feet a few more times. He heard a sudden crack and realised how easy it was to splinter a rib. And then on to his face. His mouth simply caved in, scattered, broken teeth no longer a part of it. Harold watched in surprise the vibrant red liquid oozing out of the body, forming small puddles on the pavement. But he kept on going, encouraged by his friends' cheers and the ease with which the Yid's soft, weak body was breaking.

A sudden shout came from close by, 'The police! Move it!' When he felt his right arm being forced behind his back, and heard a voice saying, 'That's enough of that, young man,' he suddenly discovered his friends were nowhere to be found. Harold was placed in a cell on his own, and even though the evidence of his aggression was smeared in red on his fists and clothes, he was only charged with 'insulting words and behaviour'.

Journalists from Corby were tipped off when it was discovered the man charged at Marylebone Police Court was 'repulsively and unbelievably a local'. Harold's picture appeared in the Corby paper. He was standing amongst a group of seventeen others, all strangers, and the title stated, 'Filthy Fascist Youth On Our Doorstep!'

Smiling proudly, Harold brought the article to his mother at the breakfast table. The anti-fascist boys had been charged the same as the fascists, but Harold wasn't sure she read that part. She glanced at the article, nodded with what he considered was approval and continued reading her letter.

Harold began to walk away when he was stopped in his tracks by his mother saying, 'I don't care what you do to the filthy Yids. I'd be happy if you got rid of a few. But for goodness' sake, Harold, try not to get arrested next time!'

2.

Kent, 7th June 1934

'Unfortunately, your mother called.' Uncle Archie told him, his pipe unlit, as ever, between his lips, where he chewed on it thoughtfully. 'I wish she'd let you be! She only comes here to bother us when she's angry or over excited about something.' He sat down and put his large, wrinkled hand on Harold's knee. 'Harold old boy, there's only a small margin of improvement if it's the latter – but that will at least give us something to be thankful for!' Archie tousled Harold's hair, a habit he'd never given up, even though Harold was a strapping young man of nineteen now.

It made Harold sad he was no longer a little lanky kid running around after his crazy uncle, with his straggly grey hair and in a t-shirt, no matter what weather, always giving time, kindness and help to one animal or another. Harold had been able to help with the animals too, without worrying about his mother. But now she was always nagging him about contributing to the household's finance. Or the least he could do, she said, was 'something about the horrible state of this country of ours.'

Harold knew she had left her large house with its well cultivated garden and cold porcelain women on the dusty mantelpieces to come to Archie's wild, tatty place for one reason only. To check up on him. The evenings here were always cold – Uncle Archie refused to light the fire to save wood for the 'real winter' which never came – mud was forever trodden in the floor, and there were never-ending soups, nettle and dandelion, cabbage, and barley, never any meat! Harold wanted more from his own life, yet he loved and understood his uncle. He was impulsive, inventive and kind; he had even found a violin somewhere and given it to Harold. He tried to play when the house was empty, but his mother's face would pop into his mind, ruining the notes. He played it when staying at the farm though; he wanted his uncle to see he did get pleasure from it.

His mother didn't even knock on the small red farmhouse door. Luckily, Harold was ready and waiting for her.

'You look almost smart,' she said, without smiling or greeting her brother-in-law. She had bought Harold the new suit, so it was barely a compliment.

Harold stood up straighter and adjusted his black tie.

'That's better.' said his mother, and sighed.

Archie put a cup of tea in front of her, with a slice of homemade cake.

'So, how are things?'

She nodded at him, and sipped her tea daintily, like a queen out of place.

Harold sat in the kitchen listening to her monologue about the jobs he should be applying for. She left soon afterwards, her cake untouched.

Archie laughed as he shut the door after her. 'What a waste of petrol. She must really love you, coming all this way just to see you off. Where are you going that's so important anyway?'

Harold put his hand on his uncle's shoulder. 'Oh, just to see if I can get myself a job in the city. I'll be back later.'

'Good luck!' Archie called after him, as he left the house.

His mother hadn't even wished him that. Harold sighed. He wanted to tell his Uncle the truth, but knew he'd disapprove. And although his mother did approve, it wasn't enough. Whatever he did would not be good enough, even if he got up onto the platform and made his own speech. He often dreamed of doing just that, his mother in the audience, clapping, cheering, with a look on her face Harold had never seen. Pride.

He checked he had the ticket one more time before he left his Uncle's farm.

Harold inspected the ticket once he was finally on the train. How were people all over the country forging them? The paper was thicker than normal, with an orangey pink background, a mixture of tea stains and orange juice. His invite had come in the post with his renewal of membership to the party, perhaps as a reward for the extra money his mother had slipped into the envelope. She'd been overjoyed he'd finally done something political – after weeks of searching the newspapers for a job, and getting increasingly frustrated with the mass of unemployment everywhere. His mother had switched on the radio, and he'd heard the incredible speech of Oswald Mosley, promising to fix the unemployment problems, and Harold had immediately joined the British Union of Fascists.

The train was slow and jolted every few minutes, but he slept almost all the way to Earls Court. It was a fitful sleep though, with unfinished dreams. He woke up feeling more tired, his mother's words ringing in his ears; 'Make sure you get off at Earls Court, and be early so you've time to get in. There will be huge queues.'

Harold walked all the way down the Warwick Road, looking at the young men loitering. Their incessant chatter suggested restlessness, but the queues were well-managed by the police, who stood idly by smoking and occasionally talking to each other and the crowds. There were people everywhere even though it was only mid-afternoon.

Harold wished he knew someone. He wasn't all that good at small talk. He stopped by three lads playing cards on a bench. They were about his age, dressed in suits and ties. For once he was glad his mother had helped him with his clothes. He leaned in closer, trying to catch their conversation.

'There will be thousands of people!' The smallest lad said, in an oddly high-pitched voice. His unruly hair fell over his eyes.

'Course there will, Phil,' replied another lad, 'There's a crisis. We're needed!'

Harold had heard the same words on the wireless: 'Crisis'.

Phil's shiny, well-combed hair and pencil moustache made him look like he was trying to be a film star. Harold wondered whether they were more serious than they sounded. He looked down the road and could just make out the curved structure of the Olympia in the distance. The queue was not moving. Perhaps he should try and find some food; he could probably eat something, though he didn't have much money. He wished he'd packed some lunch, but his stomach had protested at the thought of it.

One of the men unexpectedly turned to him and asked, 'Would you like to play cards with us? The game's better with four.'

Harold nodded and timidly introduced himself. Phil dealt the cards and they started to play. It was a good way to pass the time, and Harold began to relax.

Larger crowds were developing in small knots up and down the Warwick Road. There were uneasy murmurs.

'The reds can't have tickets.' said John, whose pug nose shone red in the sun. He had taken off his cap to wipe the sweat from his forehead.

'They don't need tickets to make trouble.' added Phil.

'Anyone would think we were frightened of them!'

Harold's confidence had been boosted by winning two games in a row. He wasn't often lucky and it gave him a rare self-assurance, and enough money to buy a couple of beers from John, who had a stash in his bag. 'The police are here, look, thousands of them, wandering around. As if we need them! The reds wouldn't dare start anything.'

Freddy, the red head, looked worried. 'If they were to stay outside... but in an enclosed hall – it could get nasty.' With utmost care, as if they were little pets, he took out a pair of steel knuckledusters from his trouser pocket. 'Shame for them,' he added, smiling triumphantly.

Harold looked Freddy up and down. He wasn't butch, and didn't seem threatening, with his freckles and little dimples even when he wasn't smiling. Would he really have the guts to use them?

The queue was moving, albeit very slowly. Harold's stomach started churning. Perhaps those beers hadn't been a good idea, after all.

Suddenly Harold saw masses of police on horseback following a growing horde of people. There were shouts of 'Down with the police!' and 'Down with...'. But before the mob had finished chanting, they were dispersed. And every time one gathered, the police broke up the ringleaders, forcing them to move.

Harold overheard one officer saying, 'Bloody troublemakers. Why can't they go back to where they came from?'

Some of the officers were sympathisers and even had tickets to come into the hall. Harold was close to the brass band playing 'Old Langsyne'. Some women in the queue were singing. A part of him wanted to stand there forever. A new era was around the corner. The words of the newspaper and the voices on the wireless were coming to life. Now he was a part of something big; he had even made friends.

Finally, they reached the entrance used for the main hall.

'Why have they only opened one set of doors?' Harold asked.

'More control on who goes in. Look how carefully they're studying the tickets.'

At the door, a tall, broad-shouldered man, in black shirt, tie and black trousers, checked each ticket. He would examine the holder from head to toe, sometimes frisking them all over, and then check the ticket once more.

All of a sudden, about a dozen people in front of them, a lad sprung out of the queue, laughing. His red tie bobbed up and down as he ran, an older man running after him, shouting, 'The wrong colour, you moron!'

A few seconds later, others ran after, with the police chasing.

Harold didn't worry when it was his turn to show his ticket. He was allowed in immediately; the man on the door gracing him with what appeared to be a smile, though it was hard to tell. He had a scar running up the left-hand side of his face and his nose was so out of joint it looked like clay.

'Another boxer,' murmured Freddy as they walked in. 'I wonder if any of the famous ones are here.'

The hall was a massive transparent cylinder, lights everywhere blinding the crowds. Harold had never seen so many people in one room. There must have been thousands making their way to the stage. It was a battle. Some were too polite to keep moving and found a spot to settle and waited.

'Come on, Harry, keep up. We're heading for the front.'

They couldn't even get halfway. There were men all over the place, positioned, it seemed, to keep order, and to ensure no one got too enthusiastic and tried to jump seats.

Harold was happy where they stopped. He wanted to be able to leave swiftly, if things got out of hand.

Nothing was happening, even though it was already past seven. There were restless murmurs from all over the hall, but they had waited all day, after all. Someone started stamping in time with the music of 'The Blackshirt's Parade' and in a matter of seconds the whole hall was full of a mesmerising rhythm. With it, Harold felt a surge of exhilaration rise from the pit of his stomach. The stamping died out quickly and the hall collapsed into a mass of incoherent murmurings again.

Harold looked around. There were young men and women in very formal wear, smart students like Harold's new friends, and conservative businessmen in stiff collar and tie, waistcoat, shapeless, baggy suits, and hats. There were families with small children. And then there were the groups closer to the platform in shabby trousers, jackets, cloth caps, and collar-less shirts.

The hall went deathly silent, and everybody stood up and watched as hundreds of flags with Union Jacks and the party's emblem swayed forward down the middle, as if they were floating. The band played a Low German march and in marched about twenty men, their boots polished and shining in the floodlights lighting their way. Four intensely bright lights were focused on the king of the evening. In answer to a fanfare, he entered the hall surrounded by officers. The whole throng cheered and saluted as one. He marched elegantly, despite his limp, his personal legacy from the trenches, with a smile of triumph. He also saluted and kept his eyes fixed in front of him; masses were gazing adoringly at him. At the platform, he turned with utmost military precision and once more made the salute. The cheers were silenced, the salute reflected by thousands, and Oswald Mosley gestured for them all to be seated.

He started his speech in deep, musical, hypnotic tones which rose with his enthusiasm. When he talked about the evil of the British financial democracy, he growled his words.

Harold could not take his eyes off this brilliant man. His ideas were inspired – surely everyone could feel it. Yet some people were being ejected from the hall.

'Down with Mosley' shouted a pretty girl who stood near him, so loudly her whole body shook. She had a red ribbon in her hair and must have been around eighteen years old.

The next moment a man about twice her size came over and struck her in the face. Harold shut his eyes too late. Was that really the only way to shut her up? And such a young, pretty girl... Those sitting nearby got ready to beat the living daylights out of her attacker, but in two seconds the approach of a dozen Blackshirts from the side of the hall put a sudden end to the whole thing. Harold shuddered to think how badly the girl had been injured.

Mosley used it to his advantage.

'We are very grateful to those few people who are interrupting. They illustrate how necessary a fascist defence force is to defend free speech in Great Britain.'

A great cheer came from the people; the victims rose like a great curtain in the hall, protecting each other.

When this had died down, Oswald's eyes followed the bleeding girl being carried out and added, 'It is typical of the red cowards to send a woman to do the job they dare not do themselves'.

The hall erupted into jeers and laughter, and Harold found himself joining in, until the sound of an ambulance stopped him in his tracks.

Mosley continued, and for a long time. Harold didn't exactly listen to the words, but he felt empowered by the rhythm of his speech.

Harold was simply swept away by the amazing spectacle of the whole event. Oswald Mosley was on a great white plinth, in the centre of the platform. He was theatrically lit up with a greyish-blue tinge. An enormous Union Jack was behind him, and he was flanked at both sides with the BUF's emblem, also draped over the microphone. When his voice boomed out the microphone, he became a god; indeed, he became the beating heart of the whole hall. Harold could pretend he was in Berlin. Mosley seemed taller than Hitler, but with the moustache, and smart suit, and the dark hair receding into his scalp, there was a definite resemblance.

The speech turned to unemployment and Harold listened eagerly. How would Mosley put an end to three million British people without jobs? He was beginning to solve the problem by forming the BUF, and paying the Blackshirts to keep order. Mosley spoke of his 'central economic theme: to advocate a policy of complete economic self-sufficiency for Great Britain and the Empire.' Harold understood there would be little need for trade with other countries – Britain would once again be a great power. Mosley explained how Britain would contain all the food, resources, raw materials, and manufacturing capacity to ensure self-sufficiency.

When Mosley introduced the importance of freedom of speech, some trouble flared up again.

'Before the organization of the Blackshirt movement' he was saying, 'free speech did not exist in this country. No great open meetings could be held. There have been cases of Reds with knives, razors, and spikes entering meetings....'

Harold glanced round at Freddy, who put his hands behind his back, shrugged and flashed him a sly smile.

'...for the purpose of denying free speech and preventing an audience of British people from discussing their problems'.

There was the unmistakeable sound of glass breaking. Immediately the commotion broke out, the Blackshirts moved in, encircled the troublemakers, and 'persuaded' them to stop.

Quite a few elderly people got out of their seats and made for the exits.

Mosley quickly tried to salvage the situation. 'Do not be alarmed, ladies and gentlemen of the party! There is a great force of Blackshirts, not only in the hall, but also surrounding it. I would never allow anything harmful to happen, and we will not give into the Reds by allowing them to violate our meeting!

Two and a quarter hours later, Mosley had summarised policies on disarmament, foreign affairs, and the National Government. It was ever so hot in the hall. When Mosley made his final point – why leave Britain unarmed so she could not defend herself? – Harold agreed wholeheartedly. But he couldn't help wondering whether Mosley had concluded his speech a little earlier than intended. A nimble climber had managed to get up to the girders, and was now shouting, 'Down with fascism!'. He was throwing pamphlets to the audience. What did he expect to achieve? People watched a procession of Blackshirts climb up to catch the communist and bring him down. Five or six men were tentatively winding their way along the girders, with thousands of spectators watching. Mosley went quiet; even his speech was not as entertaining. The men met in the centre, the communist climbed even higher above the pursuers and swung along the girders onto a platform above them. He was followed. Everyone gasped as they went out of sight.

Mosley tried to begin speaking again when a sudden crash of glass shattered the air. The communist climber had 'fallen' sixty feet at the side of the hall, those guilty of his descent still on the platform above the girders. Dignified to the end, Sir Oswald motioned for the band to play the National Anthem, and the whole hall rose together to sing. The injured person was soon forgotten in the beautifully disciplined salute and cheer ringing around the Hall; it seemed to last for minutes after Oswald left. He was followed by six men carrying the Union Jack and the British Blackshirt flag.

Harold began to follow the others making their way to the exits. He saw some of the fascists with fresh bandages on their heads. Even like this, they had sat and listened until the very end of Sir Oswald's speech.

Outside, the boys hurriedly decided which pub they were going to meet the next day. Harold was invited.

'I have to get back to work on the farm' he explained, 'It's the only job I can find at the moment. But I'll come another time.' He didn't give them his home phone number. He didn't want his mother to answer and say god knows what.

They had to move quickly; there were hundreds of police all down the road hurrying on the crowds. Lining the pavements were Communists, Pacifists, and Left-wing members of the Labour party and the I.L.P. still there with their placards and pamphlets, catcalling and booing and singing the 'Internationale'.

'Why haven't they gone home yet? Bloody Yids.' muttered John. He was the quietest of the group but outraged when he did speak. 'Why don't they just go *back* home?'

Freddy started chanting, 'Down with the Yids! Down with the Yids!'

It spread through the crowds. They continued bear baiting each other until the police broke up the glut of people. It was a strange kind of fighting, with no real attack; the Blackshirts were too strong, flooding out of the hall all together. It was a new, delicious feeling, belonging to the stronger side.

3.

London, 1940

Sir Oswald's presence at Olympia had captivated Harold. Before war broke out, he went to many meetings with his new friends. The clique looked out for him. And because they lived in East London it made sense for Harold to stay in Kent at weekends too and travel into London from there. Uncle Archie always listened to music on the wireless, never the news. And he encouraged Harold to spend as much time as he wanted with the horses. If the subject of his mother and her criticism of his joblessness was mentioned, Archie did hilarious impressions of her and told him not to worry; something would come up.

The boys managed to stay out of trouble, although Freddy often boasted about wanting it.

Harold just wanted to be noticed; perhaps he could gain promotion within the party. But it wasn't easy. That's why he had taken his chance the night of the fight in '36, the night of his arrest that was to change the course of his life forever.

*

Harold had learnt his statement by heart for the tribunal.

'I am a member of The British Union of Fascists and whole-heartedly support Hitler's intention to take over the Empire. I believe England will shortly join the fatherland, and we will live in peace and prosperity. I will never join the British army to fight against Germany.'

He looked at the row of sour-faced men sitting in their chairs, stiff and staring, judging him. What did they know? A young man on the panel afterwards even spat in his face. Surely that was against the law? But there was no point reporting it; not many people sympathised with Harold's cause. His first arrest placed him high up on the wanted list.

The smell of the cell made him ill. He already had a stomach-ache from refusing to do his business in the bucket in the corner, the one his cellmate used. The place was dark, and filthy. It was as though they'd purposely chosen the worst place this time. To teach him a lesson. And every so often there were shouts from the other inmates, 'Filthy Hitler lover!' and other pathetic insults.

No one told him for how long he would have to stay, or even spoke to him. He thought he should at least be allowed to make a phone call – but no one had come to release him even for a few minutes. Maybe they'd forgotten about him completely.

He looked at his cellmate, a hulk of a man with a hostile glare who took up half the cell. He hadn't said one word; Harold had no idea why he was there. Was he even safe?

Now, for the second time in prison, Harold had plenty of time to feel sorry for himself and to go over how the whole pitiful affair had begun. To his horror, he found himself wishing his mother and her curt tongue would come and sort it all out, even though she was to blame for the damn thing starting in the first place.

Marg Roberts

Marg's first novel, *A Time for Peace*, was published by Cinnamon Press in 2016. The novel is set in World War One Serbia where the lives of a brave Serb soldier and a British medical orderly interweave.

Marg lives in Leamington Spa with her husband and near to their family. She loves being outdoors – walking, cycling or growing plants and vegetables. Her poetry has been published in small press magazines and anthologies. In addition to poetry, she is currently writing a novel set in the 1920s race riots in Hull.

Introduction to *Making Good*

Making Good is about a relationship which has lasted 17 years. Stuart (48) and Sharon (38) lead busy lives with two teenage children. Stuart is a chef and college lecturer, and Sharon is a commis chef. On a whim – so it seems – Stuart leaves Sharon and the children.

Set in the Midlands, during a long hot summer, and following the sudden death of Stuart's mother, unresolved issues of their past catch up with them. Unless each is able to face them, their future together is threatened.

1.

Stuart sweltered in his tweed jacket and trousers under the summer's midday sun. He was hemmed in between Sharon and Eric, his dad. They had been waiting for more than five minutes, Stuart closer to his mother's coffin than he wished. He ran his palm over his head, rubbed the nape of his neck under his ponytail, aware of their kids whispering by Sharon's side. She squeezed his hand.

He smelled the freshly cut earth and listened to the roll of the distant waves, the cries of gulls, shingle and pebbles flung onto the beach where children and families played. He pictured the Irish Sea beyond the boats and oil tankers, the far blue horizon.

Yet, there was no avoiding looking down to the coffin lid. He shuddered. He licked the salt on his lips and glanced up at the group around the grave, before lowering his head again. He was a sham. He had done his best to love his mother. He remembered as a boy holding her hand, she in her navy dress and jacket, straw hat, and wishing even as a five-year-old –

she wasn't so aloof, so separate from others walking along the promenade. So far from him.

That he had to put on a show of grief he accepted, but it was hard. He wasn't the only child to feel estranged from his parents. Sharon rarely spoke of hers, hadn't attended her mother's funeral. She released his hand as if she could read his thoughts.

He heard her sigh. She smelled of his dad's kitchen soap, a skin-removing variety designed for scrubbing floors. She leaned into him, her cheek about to rest against his shoulder, till she straightened, taut, resilient.

2.

I sigh, lean against Stuart. He's not as resilient as he imagines. Cis only died last Wednesday. Why Eric didn't ring to let us know, I can't fathom. Stuart got his letter two days later, on blue, lined paper, large capitals. There were no details. Like a telegram. No consideration as to how his son might feel, or his grandkids. Stuart jumped into the car and drove straight up. I thought about her all week.

Thank God I had taken the children up at Christmas despite my cold; it being a long drive there and back in a day.

At the front door she'd looked straight past me, for Stuart I assume.

I apologised, 'He's busy at college.'

You can never tell from her face what she's thinking. 'Nice to see you all. Let's go in.'

And in she went. Into that chilly, unlit house.

While Stuart was up north with his dad, the kids and I pieced together our recollections of that last visit. Danny and Ella, despite being teenagers, had chased up and down on the beach, looked for shells, taken off their socks and paddled regardless of the cold, while I strolled with her. She'd walked well. Slowly, obviously but not breathless, no sign of pain. There'd been nothing untoward about her.

As soon as I'd handed over their Christmas presents we left the house. Eric, as usual refused to come with us. We'd gone to her favourite café. Soup and sandwiches as always. Home-made soup. Quality ham. I paid. I suspect Eric doesn't – didn't – like her spending.

The children probed each time we went up, what was Stuart like when he was little? Cis gives little away.

'Like you two, he loved the sea, he swam, collected shells and seaweed. When it was too smelly, I removed it from his bedroom, put it in the dustbin.'

'Was he ever naughty?' Ella asked.

'Never.'

Danny shook his head.

Cis added, 'He's kind. Kind to me. Always.'

She'd not seen him for 18 months. She must have missed him. She adored him; how could she not be sad he was too busy to visit? I'd felt ashamed, as if it was my fault and I ought to have made it easier for him to relax.

'As a little boy. What was the worst thing he ever did?' Danny asked.

'He's a good son,' she said.

I wonder now whether she'd some premonition, whether she was thinking about her relationship with Stuart. For when we were walking back to the house, she said, 'I think he was unhappy with us. He was different at school – not in trouble, but talkative, and he was part of a group of six boys who played together. His face changed when he walked down our path.'

'Lots of children are like that.' I tried to reassure her.

'He didn't like us.'

I could have lied, pretended some more but she wasn't a fool.

Thank God I'd tucked my arm in hers, 'We like you. Love you. You know that.'

Lovely Cis. You don't live life expecting someone you love is going to die. That makes me think of my own mum. I know she isn't going to stay much longer unremembered.

But today is for Cis. It's her funeral, Stuart's mum.

3.

Stuart hated the delay, the sense that the family was the focus of attention. To stop thinking of his mother's body disintegrating inside the coffin, he started to count the waiting mourners.

He was interrupted by Eric's announcement. 'Betty is here, vicar.'

Not before time. Whoever Betty was. A friend of his mother's, he assumed. Small, elegant and slow. No walking frame and no explanation as to why she had taken so long to walk the few yards from the church.

Bladder problem probably. The thought of ageing, as he approached fifty, filled him with dread.

The vicar fell silent as she turned from Eric, to him, to Sharon and the kids.

'Are you going to throw a flower?' Sharon was pointing to the wreaths on top of the mound of earth to the side of the grave.

He raised his eyebrows. 'What do you mean?'

A touch impatiently Sharon whispered, 'Throw a rose from your wreath onto the coffin. Yours is red.'

He was puzzled. No one had mentioned flower throwing. 'Red?'

'As a symbol of love,' Sharon urged.

'What about dad?'

'It was his idea. He's chosen freesias.'

He shook his head. It didn't feel right. His mother had hated cut flowers, hadn't she? She didn't want them in the house because it shortened their brief lives. Those they placed on his baby sister's gravestone were an exception. Gwendoline was allowed to be exempt.

His heart hammered as Sharon and the two children stepped forward. Ella's short hair was plaited. Two on each side of her head. He supposed it was cool for a kid of thirteen. Tiny red ribbons.

Very clearly, she said, 'Granny, love you,' and threw a flower.

Danny, stocky like no one else in the family, stepped forward to within inches of the grave's side. The only sound was his shirt flapping in the breeze. Stuart wondered what his son was thinking, whether this fifteen-year-old had an opinion about 'symbols of love.'

Sharon turned to him and just as quickly twisted away before crouching, letting the rose fall with a faint thud. She had loved Cis. He hoped his mother knew. He wanted to jump in the car, leave Shingle Bay and drive back to the familiar, to a different kind of tiredness, to constant adrenaline-fuelled hours. He loved teaching his students, loved his job as a chef, the way they complemented each other, but end of term was as relentless as the waves.

He unclenched his hands. Closed, opened his eyes. A woman with grey eyes was looking at him from the back of the crowd. Fiona. He remembered long hair, sleek down her back. 'Temptress,' he had whispered in her ear. He had bought her imitation Blue Grass perfume from the market.

Caught in the past, he was startled when Eric sprang from his side, as though to follow his wife into the grave. Stuart snatched at his dad's hand, but it was slapped away.

Holding aloft a spray of yellow freesias, Eric's voice trembled with the frailty of old age, 'Cis! My darling, Cis.'

His arms were raised like the crucified Christ; his head directed away from the coffin, beyond the group of mourners, towards the sky. 'I forgive you.'

Stuart, swallowing a sob, gasped, 'Dad,' appalled at the drama. His father, a reticent man, who had taught Stuart to keep his feelings to himself, was pronouncing absolution as if he were a priest. He who never went to church.

'Lass', Eric said as he finally let the flowers slip from his hand, 'Don't leave me.'

Stuart wished once more he was miles away, that they would all go, that he could be left on his own. Well, not here. Perhaps on the beach or walking along the dunes. Why did he recall at this moment, the smell of their earlier lovemaking, the yearning for their closeness to continue beyond the hotel bedroom? Flanked now by the kids and following his dad and Sharon, he listened to the roar of the outgoing tide.

4.

The kids and I reach Eric's house before the rest of the mourners. Stuart and his dad in the car behind. I hurry into the kitchen to uncover sandwiches, pizza and pork pies, and get the kids to put them on the tables in the front and living rooms.

Only when we arrived this morning after breakfast, did Stuart discover his dad had cancelled the caterers. Obviously, Eric is more shocked than we are. One week ago, he woke with his wife dead next to him. I get that. Sure, I get that. What I don't get, is that it's normal to let your son order and pay for top class caterers to deliver a funeral tea, and then to cancel it. The evening before, without telling us.

Stuart just said, 'Poor fella'.

I wanted to scream but kept quiet because Stuart was numb too. No tears – he's not the sort to cry. No word of grief about Cis, who was his mother for God's sake.

Then, who am I? No, I'm not going along that path...

I'd bought chocolate cake, lots of cakes. Not fancy like Stuart took the trouble to choose, but from the local Co-op. Stuart had wanted to give his mother a proper send-off – he's a chef after all. It's not my fault he can't. I didn't cancel the buffet. Yet, it's me he glowers at.

5.

The moment he stepped out of the funeral car Stuart wanted to drive home. Instead, he unbuttoned his jacket and hoped no one noticed him standing on the pavement. Sharon and the kids had disappeared into the house and dutifully he crossed the flagstones to join Eric, who was greeting mourners at the front door. He removed and folded his jacket, laid it along edging stones, noted the geraniums and lobelia his mother had planted in the wooden wheelbarrow.

Just for a moment, Stuart felt sad Cis wasn't there.

Even in shirt sleeves he was sweating, and he loosened his tie, stepping between his mother's planter and the narrow border. He was content to observe, hoping Eric needed no more than his presence. He noticed how expressions became serious when visitors glimpsed his dad, long-faced and morose. He was glad that nowadays most mourners resisted the temptation to wear black, wished he had stuck to the light trousers and jacket Sharon had suggested, rather than a suit Eric preferred.

'Sorry to hear of your loss,' intoned a man next in the queue to speak to Eric. He reached to shake Stuart's hand. Stuart sighed as he stepped forward. Ought he to explain, the loss was Eric's? It was hard to know how to respond, whether his 'Thank you' was enough.

The man seemed to expect nothing and by-passed Eric to step straight in the house. As Stuart listened to expressions of grief, marvelling at the number of people his parents knew, he began to wonder whether they were there out of duty or from genuine sadness. In the church there must have been a hundred, fifty at the cemetery, all of whom seemed to have accepted the invitation for a cup of tea at Eric's.

When his dad was ushered inside by a solicitous couple, Stuart again considered escaping. Would he be missed if he strolled along the beach, let his mind roll with the tide?

'She was dancing only the night before...' a white-haired woman with smudged lipstick said, dabbing her eyes. Her companion in a brightly coloured dress walked briskly towards him. 'Lovely woman,' she beamed.

The words washed over him. He stepped away from the door, tried to slip towards pavement.

'Hi, Dad!' Danny.

'Where've you been?' Stuart asked.

His son waved litre packets of milk in both hands.

Reluctantly, Stuart followed him into the house.

The front room was crowded. Judging by the emptying plates, the spread was appreciated. 'How well did you know my mother?' he was about to ask a man munching his way through a pile of sandwiches. He hesitated, realising this could be misconstrued.

Not well enough to lose his appetite for sure.

Everyone seemed to know each other, and he felt out of place. As a chef, he preferred to remain in the kitchen, as a tutor, his public role was defined. He stuffed his black tie in his trouser pocket, decided on one more attempt at leaving.

'A plate, Mr. Holmes?' A woman who reminded him of Fiona, smiled hesitantly.

He took it, nodding his thanks, grabbed an egg and cress barm cake, added a couple of sausage rolls and a few crisps, before pushing his way into the hall.

Sharon appeared in the doorway to the kitchen. The shift did little for her figure; grey aged her.

'Come and meet your mum's friends,' she said.

'How's the old fella'?' he asked.

'Standing up.'

So he should be, he thought as he followed Sharon. He bit into the sandwich.

Having rushed their hotel breakfast, they had arrived as arranged at the house at nine. His dad was nowhere to be seen.

Just before the funeral cars were due, Eric arrived in a taxi, wearing a new suit which made him look like an Italian ice-cream vendor and was waved off by three ladies. No apology. No explanation. Stuart, distraught, had just put down the phone to A and E.

Gradually, the visitors began to leave. Sharon and the kids were clearing the tables and instructed by Eric to say good-bye on his behalf at the door, Stuart was glad when he was finally alone.

He rang his boss on his mobile. There was no reply so he left a message to say he would catch up with reports by the end of the coming week. He hoped the energy to do so would return.

In the kitchen, Sharon and the kids were washing up.

'Best be off,' he said, 'when you've done.'

'Already?'

'Too much on.'

'You'd best break it to your dad.'

In the living room, Eric was sitting in one of the easy chairs in front of the electric fire. Every time Stuart saw that fire, he was irritated. Why his parents refused to have central heating installed he did not understand. He had offered to pay, as had the landlord.

Sinking into his mother's armchair, he tried to interrupt to explain why they had to go. His dad ignored him, intent on the woman sitting on the ancient settee, still wearing a black hat. He took a deep breath. Tried again, 'We're...'

'In a minute son...'

Ella and Danny rushed in carrying their cold drinks.

As she sat at the table next to Danny, Ella asked, 'Dad, why didn't you throw your flower?'

He flicked his ponytail. 'What do you mean, "my flower"?'

Just then, Sharon walked in carrying cups of tea on a tray. 'The flowers were our way of saying goodbye,' she said.

'I didn't know she was going to die, so...' He raised his arms, let them fall in frustration.

Eric said, 'A cup of tea for Betty, if you please.'

Ella went on. 'I told you, dad. The florist wrapped a red rose especially for you.'

'I don't remember.' He had no recollection of the conversation. Maybe he had been driving or was similarly distracted.

For a moment, Stuart thought Sharon was going to ignore him. Thirstier than he had realised, he jumped up to grab a cup of tea. She gave him a slight smile and sat next to Betty on the settee. Sharon was kind; she wouldn't deliberately miss him out.

Eric said, 'Son, you didn't ask Fiona to join us.'

Ready to snap, he said quietly, 'she was at the cemetery. It was up to you.'

'Who's Fiona?' Ella asked.

'My first girlfriend.' Not quite true, Irene was the first.

'Fiancée. She was a lovely girl.' His dad had been taken with Fiona; always went on about her.

'Mum's lovely too,' Ella said.

Betty joined in. A rather sharp voice. A teacher's? 'A first love is always special.'

Stuart, weary of trying to get Eric's attention, got up, his cup and saucer in his hand. 'Gotta' make a call.'

'I'll come with you,' Danny said, 'I've to ring Ethan, mum.'

'You can ring when we get home,' Stuart snapped as he hurried out of the room. In the back garden, he gulped his tea too quickly, put the cup and saucer on the path by the grass.

It was a relief to be outside. He sighed, swung his arms to and fro as he stood on the grass. He released the top button on his trousers, checked his zip and loosened the shirt from the waistband. He closed his eyes listening to the gulls. Sharon had been right. An extra night at the hotel would have helped him unwind, given her a chance to make sure his dad had shopping in, knew how to look after himself. Nonetheless, the end of term reports had to be done.

Glancing at his watch – seven already – he would give his friend, Nikki, a quick call to arrange a coffee and a chat on his way to college in the morning. A treat at the start of a busy day.

When Stuart returned to the living room, Sharon was asking Eric, 'Would you like me to give the spare sandwiches and cakes to the neighbours as a thank you for helping out?'

'If Stuart had spent the night here, instead of swanking in a hotel...' Eric began.

'You cancelled the order.'

'Leave it, Shaz.'

'If he'd been here, he'd have known what was on my mind. There'd have been no need to involve the neighbours.'

So his dad had been resentful because he had chosen to be with his family. Yet last week had gone well. They called at the GP surgery, registered Cis's death, spoke to the undertaker and the vicar. They had sorted the caterers. There had been time to relax, stroll along the beach, go out for breakfast, a slap-up meal. So why the switch in mood?

Betty shook her head, the veil like a cage over her forehead. 'That's young people for you. They're not like we were. I've told you before.'

To his surprise, Sharon persisted. 'The couple next door have grandchildren. They might be glad of a little extra.'

'Can I have a selfie of me, you and Danny?' Ella was already skipping across the room, mobile in her hand. Her chair knocked against the wall.

'Dad, I have to go. I was here all last week and there's a lot to catch up on,' Stuart said.

Eric's mouth twisted into a 'no.'

Danny righted Ella's chair. 'It's for Facebook. We put Granny on at Christmas.'

'Facebook!' Eric snorted.

'Don't you have anything to do with that nonsense,' Betty snapped.

'My Cis was on it?'

'We took the photo on the beach.'

Stuart sighed, tried once more to break into the conversation, but Danny was too quick for him. 'Granddad, you didn't want to come. It was too cold for you.'

'Let me see.' Eric leaned forward as Ella flipped through images on the screen.

Stuart raised his voice slightly. 'Okay, kids! Time to go.' He looked to Sharon for support; she was watching Ella.

Eric was scratching his chin. 'I didn't know you could do that. Doesn't she look grand?'

'I'll take one of you so all my friends can see you as well,' Ella said.

He might as well not exist. Ella was pointing out the lens to Eric before saying, 'Smile, Granddad.'

Stuart reached a hand to Sharon and pulled her to her feet. 'We must get going. I'm shot.'

Half an hour later, they reached the front door. His dad shook his hand. 'Couldn't have managed without you.'

Sharon was loaded up with leftovers they wouldn't eat. Some exchange had gone on between her and Eric. Too shattered to ask, he watched her slam the boot shut. Her face set, she alone didn't wave to his dad standing next to Betty on the step.

6.

It was gone eight when they reached the outskirts of Shingle Bay. It being Friday, the road leading to the motorway was packed in both directions. Stuart slipped on a Garth Brooks CD. The slow opening notes soothed his jangled mind.

'Boring,' Ella said.

'You've got your own.'

'I told you. I forgot my headphones.'

He switched it off, not wanting her to spoil his listening. Ella used to stay awake so he could kiss her goodnight, but nowadays if she glanced at him when he came into the room, he was lucky.

'I used to like the end of term,' he said putting his foot down as the traffic speeded up.

Sharon nodded. 'I know.'

He sighed. It didn't help that he combined two jobs – he didn't have to worry about his work as a chef till the middle of the week, but he was daunted by the concentration needed to complete the college reports. Involuntarily he snorted.

'What are you laughing at?' Ella demanded.

Too tired to correct her, he said, 'Granddad nearly falling in the grave.'

She punched the back of his seat. 'You're cruel.'

He couldn't expect her, any of them really, to understand. Last week he had enjoyed Eric's company; he had listened to stories about the goings-on at The Grand where he and Cis had worked and had reciprocated with incidents from the kitchen at La Marmite, exaggerated of course. Today the relationship had reverted to its disappointing norm.

The static from Danny's headphones, the whoosh of a Porsche flying along the fast lane, increased his irritation. He ought to let Sharon drive.

Again, the punch on his seat. 'We must invite granddad to stay during the hols.'

'We're going camping.'

'He's ever so lonely, Da-ad.' Her pleading became a whine.

'Lonely isn't how I'd describe him.'

As they drew towards the M6 intersection he slowed, glancing at the sign to Lancaster and the Lakes. No doubt about it, he had been relieved to wave goodbye to his dad. The man thought he was the centre of the world. His mother had fussed after him, never disagreeing. She had once nodded her approval while he lectured on the unnecessary drama that women made of childbirth. Both his mother and Sharon had remained silent.

'Betty and his other friends will visit,' Danny was explaining to Ella on the back seat. 'She told me they will take care of him.'

Glancing in the wing mirror as traffic exited to services, he signalled to overtake a convoy of lorries, vigilant for some idiot to shoot into his lane. No one understood what his parents had been like during his childhood. Though they didn't neglect him, nor cause him deliberate harm, he had been miserable.

'Shall we take the toll road?' Sharon asked.

'When we get there.'

He ought to have stuck up for Sharon when his dad was rude to her. Today especially. The success of the funeral tea had been due to her. Organising, shopping. Had he been weary or mean-spirited? Sometimes he enjoyed, revelled in her discomfort. He cast her a sideways glance. Sighed.

As soon as he slipped into the rhythm of driving, he relaxed. He was careful especially with the kids in the back; he checked the mirrors, kept within the limit despite the temptation to speed. He sometimes wondered if he wasn't a mite too responsible. What he would really like to do was travel up to Scotland, maybe to one of the remote islands. Of course, he wouldn't, couldn't. Cedric needed his reports and François, expected him to work his full quota from Wednesday till the annual closure, a week tomorrow.

'Will you check the tents while the weather holds?' Sharon asked.

'If there's time.'

It had been raining when they got home last August and Nikki (he could hardly describe her as a lover) had rung, suggesting they met for a coffee. Her invitation had felt exciting, made him feel special though the holiday had gone well.

Sharon interrupted his thoughts. 'Where do you fancy?'

'What about granddad?' Ella said. 'When's he coming to stay?'

'If we tried the Lakes, we could call on the way up.'

Danny dropped his headphones on his lap. 'Don't forget my football training.'

'You'll not be camping with us?' Stuart teased, his humour improving.

The family lived for the three weeks' camping. On holiday he loved them all. Little was planned. They played on the beach, swam in the sea, cooked improvised meals on the barbecue or played games or sang round a fire. Maybe it was the unexpected that appealed. Sharon stuck to her one glass of wine each night, but with three or four beers inside him, the fresh air, the kids' laughter, Sharon's body curled round his in the tent, he became himself again.

'If it stops granddad staying, it will be best if we don't go camping.' Ella spoke as if the decision rested with her.

Sharon twisted to face her daughter. 'Do you have something else on?'

'It's not just me. Danny has stuff as well.'

The idea of waking up with Eric in their house appalled him. Every day given to trying to please him, and watching his face shrivel when it didn't, and yet the last week, with just the two of them, their relationship had become close.

'It's not about granddad, it's about you, isn't it?' Sharon asked.

'He's old and lonely and granny has just died. It's only fair.' Ella's voice rose.

'He's not coming. End of.' Stuart snapped. Ahead the gantry indicated a lane closure and speed restriction ahead. He swerved into the fast lane. One week to endure and then their annual holiday.

Michael Toolan

Michael Toolan taught English language and literature for many years at universities in Singapore, Seattle, and latterly Birmingham, where he now lives and writes long and short fiction. Recent stories have appeared in the annual short fiction anthologies of the Scottish Arts Trust (*A Meal for the Man in Tails*, 2021, and *Beached*, 2022); in Litro online magazine (May 2023); and In *Oluwale Now* (Peepal Tree Press, Summer 2023). He is revising a second novel while seeking representation for his first, *Term of Adjustment*. What follows is the opening of that novel.

In the Admin Building
Monday 5th October, 8:15am

Emma Winchester, attractive, clever, and well-paid, with a stylish apartment and a cheerful temperament, enjoys a lifestyle that ticks all her boxes and has reached the age of thirty-seven with very little to cause her serious stress. Take her job: she is Pennington University's Head of External Relations and loves every minute of it. Pumped after her early-morning workout at the gym, she has been in her office in the Admin building since 8, barrelling through the emails that have come in overnight. Dodging the worst of the traffic by getting in early, she has parked her top-of-the-range BMW Coupé at the back of the Admin block, quietly exulting in being one of the special few with a reserved space on campus.

Emma and Pro Vice-Chancellor Joe Dunne are about to have a quick pre-meet with the boss, Vice-Chancellor Derek Marsh, as soon as he is in his office. She has just seen him being dropped at the front of the Admin building by Reg, his driver, delaying a wheelchair-using member of staff rolling towards the ramped access. She knows Reg will have collected Derek about ten minutes ago from his official residence a mile away from campus, Mattersley Court: an elegant late-Victorian villa adjoining sports fields also owned by the university and set in grounds so extensive they require a full-time gardener.

While Reg is parking the Jag, Emma watches Derek skip up the front steps, her heart giving a little lurch of anxiety and pleasure. He nods and smiles at everyone he passes, his fashionably shaven head setting off his lean, tanned features. He looks fresh as a daisy, eager to throw himself into another intense week of meetings and troubleshooting, although she knows he only got back from Montreal on Saturday. He's wearing one of his Paul Smith suits — lightweight, navy — and it fits his long muscular frame perfectly. With the primrose shirt and feisty-looking silk tie — some sort of abstract collage, with Rorschach splodges of grey, vermilion, and ultramarine — the ensemble works surprisingly well. There's something vigorous and springy in the way he carries himself; working with him gives her a huge buzz. But she senses difficult situations ahead. Not in the job, God no, but in their personal relations. Difficult, but interesting too, she has to admit; exciting even.

The Vice-Chancellor's office
Monday 5th October, 8:30am

Why July?, Vice-Chancellor Derek Marsh asks. Emma is more than ready for this one.

— Dinford Bogle Smith, who did the market research, calculate early July is now the peak month for sixth-formers wanting to visit universities and make their choice of preferred HE destination. Plus, she adds, counting these factors off on her fingers, the campus looks its best then, any students still around are post-exams and much more relaxed, the Sports Centre and the library and food outlets are far less crowded than usual, staff are more available...

As she speaks, Emma admires the natural poise with which Derek sits forward attentively. He looks ready to pounce, it occurs to her, not unpleasantly.

— OK, says Derek. I suppose we can make sure there's no date clash with the degree ceremonies?

— Actually I had a different thought about that, says Emma. I mean what could be nicer for Mum and Dad and their teenager than seeing all those proud parents spilling out of the Great Hall onto the lawns with *their* just-graduated son or daughter, all dressed up in gown and mortar-board? And then catching a glimpse of some honorary graduand like David Harewood or Gareth Southgate circulating in the fizz and strawberries marquee...

— Nice, nice, I like it, says Derek. Have we approached Southgate, by the way? It'd be good to get him while the team's still doing ok ...

Derek and Emma are reviewing the plan she will present to the university's Executive Committee, the Ex-Co, tomorrow. It's a new initiative called The Pennington Showcase: a week of campus talks, performances, and interactive events, to be run next summer and aimed as much at the general public as any students, mostly graduate, still around then. The Showcase is intended to 'enrich the university's offer', especially its appeal to students who've just done their AS's and are on the point of deciding which universities to apply to.

Joe Dunne is also present: besides being Pro Vice-Chancellor for Sciences he has the remit of overseeing Student Satisfaction. A fourth person ought to be attending: the university's Head of Admissions, Steve Boniface. But after many months off sick with stress Steve's early retirement on medical grounds has gone through. His post is being advertised, and Derek doesn't rate the woman acting up, so hasn't asked her to this meeting.

— You're suggesting a mix of talks and activities, Derek continues. Presentations from our medics, playwrights, chemists, musicians...

— I like the one where the Politics lecturers use Drama students in scenes illustrating contemporary issues, Joe enthuses. Carbon-dependence, meat-eating, sexual harassment, Scottish independence. They should work really well.

— Hmm. Nothing too daft and socialist I hope, says Derek, chuckling to soften his tone.

— Or daft and little Englander, Joe counters, holding in check his irritation at Derek's jibe.

— I don't want anything that makes parents think we'll turn their kids into professional activists Derek says firmly, blanking Joe and addressing his remarks to Emma.

— Exciting ideas harnessed to material success and good citizenship, he continues. That's the narrative.

— Absolutely, Emma agrees. So we've got Sally Proctor and her film clips about the new drugs they're exploring for Parkinson's sufferers: we'd schedule her for one of the peak time-slots. She connects so well with audiences ...

— I'm glad you've included Materials Science, Joe says, pointing a stubby finger at an item in Emma's document.

— What are they going to do?, Derek asks.

— Something about their low-carbon process for converting old tyres and reclaimed plastic into an aggregate for the new cycle-paths around town... quite impressive really.

— Appeals enormously to the sixth-formers, and their parents too, Emma says.

— What about the Humanities?, Derek asks. What fascinating and inspirational talks about their work's impact in the real world will they offer, I wonder?

Privately Derek thinks most of the research and publishing done by his Arts and Humanities staff is about as important as interior design or flower-arranging. Still, there are several thousand suckers willing to pay more than £9k a year to be taught by them, thank you very much.

— It's trickier, says Emma, who shares Derek's general attitude to the Humanities. I mean, she continues, a talk about racism in Shakespeare or gender fluidity in the novels of Virginia Woolf isn't going to cut it. The History and Law talks are better, because they usually tell a proper story. But the

Literature and Modern Languages departments do struggle to come up with topics that seem relevant to a general audience...

— For some reason, Derek adds, exchanging a broad grin with Emma.

— Well, says Joe, and then stalls.... He wants to speak up for these staff that, whatever their failings, he regards as decent and hardworking. People like Rhona Fielding, far more nurturing of their students than the typical Science staff. And maybe doing more good. Take this Parkinson's breakthrough of Sally Proctor's: a drug that would be cheaper and easier to take than Levodopa, helping the brain with its stop-start instructions to the limbs and muscles. Fair enough, and in time, maybe many thousands of folk with Parkinson's will live a bit longer and a bit more comfortably than before. But what will they *do* with the extra time and better quality of life? That's where the Arts come in, he reckons.

While Joe has been thinking all this, Derek has been holding forth:

— One does wonder what the point is of some of what they get up to. Every discipline has its own preoccupations, of course, and as a university in the original sense of the word we want to support the full range of important branches of intellectual enquiry.

— Tosser, Joe thinks.

— Different academic subjects have their own ways of developing, driven by scientific breakthroughs, new technology, paradigm shifts...

Emma and Joe stay silent, knowing to wait until Derek has shared his thoughts, with whatever hints about longer-term plans they might contain.

— But look at how Deconstructionism was all the rage twenty-five years ago in the Humanities, and now it's totally ignored or obsolete, as far as I can see.

Emma chuckles her agreement, although she knows no more about deconstructionism than the other two.

— And I don't think our Showcase would benefit from a talk on the deconstruction of deconstructionism, Derek quips.

Joe laughs too, this time.

— But what is the dominant approach now? What they do is all over the place intellectually, thoroughly eclectic. And the younger Historians are just as bad.

At this point Derek shuts up, knowing from long experience that saying less may save him from boxing himself in. For all he knows, this very month someone in the English Department may have charmed Leverhulme or the Arts Research Council into forking out serious money, a six-figure sum, to support a project revisiting one of these hyper-intellectual traditions. God knows what's in fashion these days in the Humanities. But he can safely predict it will involve one of the big guilt trips they never tire of: racism, sex- and gender-discrimination, or colonialism. These still seem to drive most of the impenetrable 'research' done in the Humanities.

— OK says Derek, wrapping things up. I think we have the makings of a really strong pitch, demonstrating the range and ambition of the activity constantly in train at Pennington.

Let's put it to the Ex-Co for their approval of the, what did we calculate, £100k budget?

— That's correct, Vice-Chancellor.

— Right. Money well spent, if it gets us over the tipping point with a few strong applicants looking at Manchester or Birmingham as their first choice. Thank you Emma, Joe.

With that, the pair leave Derek's inner sanctum, exchanging a quick professional smile with Tricia, Derek's devoted secretary in the outer office, on their way. Emma returns to her own office along the corridor, while Joe heads across campus towards the Chadwick Building, where he has a spartan office amongst the Physicists, rather than be seduced by the corporate plush of the senior managerial suite in the Admin block. He is briefly absorbed in the throng of staff and students heading in every direction. Among these he notices a smartly-dressed man of Middle-Eastern appearance approaching the revolving door of the Modern Languages building. More likely a lecturer than a mature Ph D student coming in this early, Joe thinks, and a reasonably affluent one too, judging by his clothes. Is that jacket mohair?, he wonders.

Actually Joe has had just as early a start as Emma off at her gym. By seven o'clock as usual, he had put the lead on Arthur and taken him "for a walk and a crap" as he liked to say, much to his wife Maureen's disapproval. Soon he had done the needful with one of the plastic bags he kept in his jacket pocket. No-one liked shovelling shit, Joe had reflected, resigned to doing just that every day. Worse than shovelling, he corrected himself, grunting involuntarily while reaching down to grasp Arthur's hot brown turds, mercifully firm, through the flimsy transparent plastic. What must other cultures think of this practice, he had often wondered: the Indians of high caste or low for that matter, or the Arabs? Let alone our own medieval forebears: they'd have laughed their heads off.

Still, he was fond of Arthur (named for Scargill, not the Camelot king), a brown-coated Staffie bull terrier. An early morning half-hour out and about in Arthur's company always gave the day a bit of perspective. On his way around the park he would exchange a few words with other dog-walking regulars, a nod or a smile with passing joggers. Often as not these were fresh-faced young women, running in pairs in figure-hugging tops and leggings, a pleasing prospect. A small uplifting moment of social connection, as well as low-impact exercise, good for mind and body. Then back home for a simple breakfast of toast and coffee, sometimes a bit of fruit, before he quickly attended to his own needs ("oh give it a rest, Joe!" Maureen would complain). Today, changed into his suit, he had walked again, dogless this time, for the twenty-five minutes it took to get to campus, trying to keep his mind off his To Do list, but with limited success.

What he couldn't block out entirely were gloomy thoughts about his own insecure administrative position, as one of Derek Marsh's Pro Vice-Chancellors. He was increasingly unhappy with Derek's preoccupation with market-minded business principles, and suspected a conspiracy was afoot, to remove him from the senior management team. That would dump him back in his Department where, at this stage in his career, he had no role. But there was no way around it: in terms of what Derek expected from the members of the executive committee, Joe knew the cut of his jib didn't suit. The corporate-speak and 'managing exits' and measurable targets were only part of it. Even the fact he lived within walking distance of the campus was a mark against him, implying far too much commitment to the university as distinct from the job. All the other P V-Cs had their real home elsewhere, some comfortable residence in Cambridge or London or the Peak district, where their real life would run smoothly on if a bigger post moved them to Birmingham or wherever. Sometimes he felt he was in a minority of one among those with any influence, although he had taken some comfort from finding that a few others, like Brian Smiles on the University Council, also had reservations about the corporate emphasis. Well, he had concluded as he reached the Admin Building in good time for the Showcase meeting, there wasn't much he could do except wait for Derek to make his move.

For the record, let us note that neither Emma nor Joe has had anything like the early start of the gaggle of people to be seen around nine o'clock labouring against the incoming flow, walking away from campus towards the bus stops. Most are mature women in dark clothing, seemingly of North African or Middle Eastern heritage, sometimes with just their brown faces showing; they are too motherly in appearance to be entirely at home on a university campus. Some walk alone and silently, blank-faced with fatigue; all proceed slowly, as if glad they will soon be off their feet, while talking animatedly in twos and threes. Several are on their phones, shouting almost (one of the women, speaking Somali, is asking her interlocutor if he remembered to give Abty money for the school visit to the aquarium). They don't look like students, or the early morning users of the sports centre. Of course! They're a detachment of the army of contract cleaners, heading home or to their next part-time job, content that another three hours of work has been completed, another £27 earned. Most of the university's cleaners work like this, hired in from an outside company. Only a few of the longest-serving staff, now nearing retirement, have managed to stay on under the old terms that include sick pay and annual leave; they're the ones you see pottering around campus during the normal working day.

Forty minutes after Joe and Emma have returned to their offices, if you are in the Partridge Rotunda on the top floor of the university's Administration building and looking south, beyond the campus, to the busy Leicester Road, you will see a gaggle of students, mostly female and mostly Asian, tumbling noisily off the number 53 bus which has stopped near the university's South entrance.

Near the front of this delegation is a young woman, scarcely distinguishable from the others in her dark coat, dark hair and purple scarf. At this distance she is really only remarkable for her colourful backpack, an ornate symmetrical Eastern design, possibly floral in inspiration. This is Asma Usmani, a final year BA English Literature student. She is walking faster than the others, because she is only just in time for the 10 a.m. lecture in her Romanticism module, which has a promising title she thinks: *Shelley: radical, decadent, or both?* We'll hear more about Asma in due course.

One of the tutors on that Romanticism module is Professor Rhona Fielding, but you'll never catch her giving the lecture on Shelley, that chancer. Right now, her hair still damp from her early morning swim in the university sports centre pool, she is making PowerPoint slides for her final year class on 'Identity politics in modern film and literature'. She has taken the dull official module description and inflected it with a more engaging emphasis: a special focus on women poets' and filmmakers' re-fashioning of their identities in a digital world. The lecture she is preparing will talk about this as a significant new sociocultural form of urban modernity, alongside some of the movements that contest or even oppose it, such as the patriarchal, heteronormative and misogynistic worldviews of Trumpian populism and radical Islam, to take two recent examples. It's a big topic, Rhona realises, and in her fifty-minute lectures and even the follow-up two-hour weekly seminar she can only scratch the proverbial surface. The surface, she thinks: that which since Baudrillard and Instagram we have learned to worship... *Down with depth!*, it now occurs to her, might make a good lecture title some day.

On this occasion, scratching the surface involves a sampling of work and responses to it in Anglo-American film and literary culture. So today's slides are simple pointers to the main arguments in the dense set readings from Butler, Crapanzano, and Pratt; plus enlivening stills and video clips from Kurosawa,

Dana Rotberg, Zhang Yimou, and poets performing their own work. She chafes against this reducing of complexity to bite-sized chunks, mostly visual.

Still, the students like her classes — more than like, they love them. She has them eating out of her hand in seminars. True, their contributions are often quite 'random', to use their own word. But they evidently find the course material very 'relatable' (another of their words: horrible!), presumably because it is about the things they are grappling with in their own lives: in essence, how to be happy in your own skin. As if, even in her fifty-fifth year, turning away from her computer screen and looking out of her open office window to admire the perfect physique of a vigorous young Mellors in a clingy green T-shirt who is riding a sit-on mower and giving the lawn a final autumnal treatment, taut stomach muscles rippling and shoulders flexing as he makes each 180° turn, back and forth, back and forth, smooth stroke after smooth stroke, the steady drone of the machine reaching her together with the gladdening smell of cut grass, she has the answer to that one.

At the Book Club
Monday 5th October, 11am

Rhona and her students are not the only ones in Pennington using literature this morning to explore how to be happy in your own skin. You can add Alison Marsh and Maureen Dunne, wives of the Vice-Chancellor and Joe Dunne respectively, for a start. It is mid-morning, and after a couple of hours rushing around completing household and family chores, Maureen and Alison are settled in the bosom of the monthly book club. Today it is at Jenny Pyle's house.

Alison and Maureen have become quite close over the past year, particularly now that Maureen has retired from teaching and can get to the morning meetings of the book group. Most people connected to the university keep Alison at a distance, making her feel like a respected but irrelevant appendage, her previous career as a civil servant counting for nothing. Not with Maureen, thankfully. But then their friendship stems from this book club really, and not so much from the university.

Today the group are discussing a much-loved campus novel classic, David Lodge's *Nice Work* — a lighter choice for the autumn which everyone agreed on "because you can't be reading heavy stuff by David Foster Wallace and Clarice Lispector the whole time can you?". Jenny Pyle, their host, is quietly pleased everything is going so well. Dressed simply in tailored orange chinos and a floral blouse half-hidden by a Liberty print apron, she is standing at the centre of her large conservatory, armed with a two-litre cafetière and rotating slowly to offer re-fills. Around her a dozen women have distributed themselves casually but not without some sense of occasion, in a variety of cushioned rattan sofas and armchairs.

They are a fine gathering of educated, articulate women, capable and productive; and they know it, in a contented way which is not overly self-congratulatory, they feel. Like the splendid cacti amongst which they sit, they can be prickly and are tougher than they look — as you'd expect in women who've either retired early or cut back their working hours in demanding jobs. All are dressed interestingly and expensively: Jigsaw and up, as it were. All are in their fifties, low sixties tops, and nearly all keep themselves in shape on a scale you would rate from reasonable to impressive. But for the fact they'd turn on such a person and denounce them as a sexist ageist worm, anyone might remark they are still sexually attractive.

Look at Alison Marsh, for example: in her mid-fifties, she could easily pass for a decade younger, with her trim figure thanks to cross-country skiing at Christmas and tennis holidays in the shoulder months on the Algarve and, most of all, year-round swimming and Zumba. If some of the others have weight worries, these don't deter them from enjoying the home-baked *pains aux raisins* with their second cups of Jenny's exceptional Colombian coffee (Alec brought it back from Bogota, isn't he clever? Apparently you can get it here sometimes at *À Table!*). This is the coffee break before the discussion: they always start with the break rather than the book, an old joke they never tire of.

While Debs is asking Jenny how she manages to get her fig tree to do so well in the conservatory, Maureen turns to Ali and says:

— You know I was looking through *Nice Work* again and it occurred to me there isn't a single mention of the Vice-Chancellor.

— Really? Let me think.... You know I think you're right, I can't remember any either. Well...not as a character we learn anything *about*. It's just the Vice-Chancellor's office that orders Robyn and Vic to pair up on that work exchange, isn't it? Industry and academia.

— Yes. The Shadowing business, Maureen says.

— But we get absolutely no sense of the Vice-Chancellor as a person. As if back then they were marginal to a campus novel.

— Exactly. No personal mentions at all. Or of the Vice-Chancellor's wife, for that matter. Or perhaps I should say the spouse. Partner.

— Well, yes, I suppose so! But even today the V-C's partner *is* usually a wife, isn't ....she?

— But *why* isn't there any mention of the V-C in those campus novels?

— Yes, it's something to think about isn't it? I would say that in my experience Vice-Chancellors are not all that, you know, *humanly interesting*, in the way that Lodge makes Robyn and Vic interesting. Maybe they don't have foibles the way.... well, that's daft, everyone has their own oddities if you dig deep enough.

Maureen smiles and sips her coffee but says nothing.

— But I would say that V-Cs are not in themselves amusing, or a vehicle for irony. Neither a source nor a cause of comedy, intentional or unintentional.... It's OK to laugh, Maureen!

They both do. Maureen gasps a 'sorry' but Ali says:

— No, no, I'm not being disloyal to Derek. It's not him particularly, it's all of them, believe me!

Soon the official discussion of the follies of Vic and Robyn and Morris Zapp starts up, so their private conversation goes no further. But sharing some of their thoughts with the group, Maureen wonders if there isn't a kind of innocence and even an irresponsibility about the doings of Vic and Robyn in the long-ago 1980s.

— Yes, I think there is, says Erica. Those were the days before computing arrived and then the internet and digital everything and now social media, colonising every part of human life.

Ali ventures that what Maureen called the innocence of Robyn and Vic is also part of their charm.

— They can't really *hurt* anyone, except a loved one emotionally of course, Alison continues. Unlike a Vice-Chancellor today, Lodge's characters have little real power over other people's livelihoods or sense of self-worth. They certainly don't have control over the course of a very large enterprise, whose initiatives and 'rationalisations' are under public scrutiny. Or thought to be. Universities in campus novels back then look like a different animal from what they actually are now.

A brief silence follows.

— Well, says Fiona McAndrew, to borrow a familiar phrase, you may very well say so Ali; I couldn't possibly comment.

Everyone laughs, glad of this release of the slight tension Alison's remarks have created. Some of the women are uncomfortable with her dose of Op-Ed, which to them sounds critical of modern universities even though, as the wife of a Vice-Chancellor, she has far more of an interest, a pecuniary interest even, than anyone else present — including Maureen. Others are not so much uncomfortable as annoyed, suspecting Ali to be claiming insider expertise, when as far as they are concerned she is just a spouse and beneficiary of Derek's position.

Neither of these reactions surfaces in the conversation, however, because Philippa takes over the topic:

— I agree there is a difference between then and now, or the fictional then and the real now, but I don't think it's so extreme. Take Vic, for example: he's got his business, very much in his hands, so he does have some power over the staff he employs.

— True, says Ali, but he is pretty powerless, isn't he? When he loses contracts to rival firms, he tries to act for the best, but he has no power to change the situation.

Fiona, a retired secondary school head-teacher now keeping busy as a magistrate (she has only had to withdraw from sittings twice so far, when former pupils were up on charges of dealing and assault), very much agrees:

— He's a middle-manager. But being 'old school' he sees those who work under him as his responsibility rather than just dispensable. The head office he answers to is 'new school' by comparison, as we see at the end when he gets fired.

— Likewise with Robyn, Erica adds. The grades she gives and the references she writes presumably have some effect on her students' prospects, but she is only doing what the wider community expects her to do. Neither she nor Vic can really control much of anything in their world, even though they evidently want to. I suppose that dissonance can create comedy.

— Or tragedy?, Maureen queries.

— Absolutely, says Debs. We do need to think about genre here. You know: what Lodge had in mind. I'd say it's a kind of playful hybrid: part romance, part state of the nation realism, part satire... ivory tower meets brick factory chimney...

— Ooh that's good Debs, says Erica cheerily.

— And it has a bitter pill in it, Fiona adds, about industrial decline and ruthless competition, dirty competition even, like the tricksiness to do with academic posts. But overall if we're thinking about genre, it makes me think of a lovely saying they have in Belfast. (Fiona's distant roots are Ulster Presbyterian, an interesting contrast with Maureen's equally distant Cork Catholicism; far from this causing difficulties, they have a kind of affinity, knowing each other's backgrounds so well). *Catch yourself on!* they say. It means something like listen to yourself, see how stupit you're being! (Fiona's posh accent has turned a little Belfast during these last phrases; she really does say stupit).

— Well, says Ali, all I'm saying is perhaps there simply isn't much scope for, you know, entertaining but instructive exposure of human folly blah blah blah .... anywhere near a university administration building. In a novel I mean. Back then or, even more so, nowadays. It would just be too humdrum, all their committee meetings and targets and spreadsheets. It's all a bit flat and procedural.

— But surely you're not saying that Vice-Chancellors aren't fully-rounded human beings, are you Ali?

An alert silence follows.

— Well I'm not sure I'd go that far!, Ali responds. But look at Philip Swallow and Robyn and Morris Zapp—always in the thick of things, full of venal impulses, petty rivalries and prickly sensitivities. Whereas the modern Vice-Chancellor is so removed from all that kind of, you know, sexual tension and back-stabbing and intimacy. Maybe his detachment goes along with his enormous salary—

— Or hers, these days, says Midge.

— Or hers, true. I do think their salaries and perks make a huge difference. It separates them from the staff and students. Even the ones with a social conscience. They bang on a lot about giving back, charitable giving and so on. But there's quite a lot of resentment that while the ordinary staff pay their taxes, Vice-Chancellors get to be philanthropists! Derek doesn't like me saying this but I'm sorry, it's what I feel.

The discussion surges and stalls by turns, animated by voices raised and people almost rudely interrupting each other, then at other times hesitant and intermittent, dwindling to periods when no-one at all speaks and you can hear a stifled yawn or someone saying 'hmm' *sotto voce*, as if the room has morphed into a Quaker meeting.

When the talk resumes, all agree that the set piece where Robyn visits the factory is brilliant.

— It's so graphic and visceral! As if she had wandered innocently into a scene of nightmarish industrial violence...

— I *know*.... The suppressed aggression, the deafening noise...

— But it was the reality, wasn't it, not just in Vic's factory but in hundreds of factories here where tens of thousands of people spent their entire working lives. And Robyn stumbles in there with *no idea* of how ghastly everyday work was for so many people.

— The cruellest of the irony was that these hellish factories like Vic's were closing because of cheaper and *more hellish* factories in Korea or China or wherever. And Vic like most people was *appalled* to see the businesses going under...

No-one can think of anything to add on this depressing topic, so Jenny suggests they wrap up the discussion of *Nice Work*, adding:

— I did want to say how much I enjoyed the way the novel begins, mostly in Vic Wilcox's thoughts, worrying about his job and his wife going through the menopause ...

— It's a convincing picture of the modest consumerism around 1980, don't you think? Before computers and the internet and smartphones. Not the nouveau riche but the nouveau affluent, I suppose, and worried about maintaining it in a cut-throat world...

— I wonder if some of us aren't, in effect, the children of Vic and whatshername, Fiona remarks.

— Marjorie.

— Of course, Marjorie.

— How do you mean, Fiona?, Jenny asks.

And off they go again.

Milton Keynes UK
Ingram Content Group UK Ltd.
UKHW020645291123
433416UK00018B/1328